THE DOUBLE TONGUE

When William Golding was awarded the Nobel Prize
in Literature, the Nobel Foundation said of his novels
that they 'illuminate the human condition in the world of
today'. Born in Cornwall in 1911, Golding was educated
at Marlborough Grammar School and Brasenose College,
Oxford. Before becoming a writer, he was an actor, a lec-
turer, a small-boat sailor, a musician and a schoolteacher.
In 1940 he joined the Royal Navy and saw action against
battleships, submarines and aircraft, and also took part in
the pursuit of the *D*̶ ̶ ̶ ̶ ̶

Lord of the ̶  ̶ ̶ ̶ d by several
publishers and ̶ ̶ ̶ ̶ ed from the
'slush pile' by ̶ ̶ ̶ er and published in 1954. eral million
copies; it was translated into 35 languages and made into a
film by Peter Brook in 1963. He wrote eleven other novels,
The Inheritors and *The Spire* among them, a play and two
essay collections. He won the Booker Prize for his novel
Rites of Passage in 1980, and the Nobel Prize in Literature
in 1983. He was knighted in 1988. He died at his home in
the summer of 1993.

www.william-golding.co.uk

Books by
Sir William Golding
1911–1993
Nobel Prize in Literature

Fiction

LORD OF THE FLIES

THE INHERITORS

PINCHER MARTIN

FREE FALL

THE SPIRE

THE PYRAMID

THE SCORPION GOD

DARKNESS VISIBLE

THE PAPER MEN

RITES OF PASSAGE

CLOSE QUARTERS

FIRE DOWN BELOW

TO THE ENDS OF THE EARTH

(comprising *Rites of Passage, Close Quarters* and *Fire Down Below* in a
revised text; foreword by the author)

THE DOUBLE TONGUE

Essays

THE HOT GATES

A MOVING TARGET

Travel

AN EGYPTIAN JOURNAL

Plays

THE BRASS BUTTERFLY

LORD OF THE FLIES

adapted for the stage by Nigel Williams

WILLIAM GOLDING: A CRITICAL STUDY OF THE NOVELS

by Mark Kinkead-Weekes and Ian Gregor

WILLIAM GOLDING

The Double Tongue

faber and faber

First published in 1995
by Faber and Faber Limited
Bloomsbury House, 74–77 Great Russell Street,
London WC1B 3DA
This paperback edition first published in 2013

Typeset by Faber and Faber Ltd

Printed and bound by CPI Group (UK) Ltd, Croydon, CR0 4YY

A CIP record for this book is available from the British Library

ISBN 978-0-571-29853-2

2 4 6 8 10 9 7 5 3 1

Publisher's Note

At the time of his sudden death at his home in Cornwall in June 1993 William Golding had completed two drafts of this novel, and he was about to begin a third. From his working notes, and references in his Journal right up to the day before he died, it appears that the draft which we publish here had more or less the form of the novel he planned to send to his publishers in the autumn of the year. It would almost certainly have been longer, as the other, more unfinished, draft was, but from the notes and his own comments written on the typescript the characterization of the Pythia herself seems to have been largely settled. He rewrote the beginning of the story a number of times, and we print what we take to be one of the latest versions of the opening pages found among his papers. Apart from Lady Golding, to whom he read the passages about the meeting of the Pythias and the bookroom, he showed the working texts to no one. He typed both the drafts himself. *The Double Tongue* has been chosen as a title by the editors from among several others in his handwriting at the head of the drafts. He used these titles variously in his Journal during the six months he was writing the book.

The author's family
wish to dedicate his last work
to all those at Faber
who helped, encouraged and cared for
him and his writing
over the past forty years.
Above all, this book is for

CHARLES

Introduction by Meg Rosoff

In the city of Delphi on the side of Mount Parnassus, a specially selected priestess (Pythia) descends into an underground chamber to put questions to the god Apollo. The god's prophecies emerge from the Pythia's mouth in babbling riddles, which the High Priest of Apollo 'translates' for supplicants from all corners of the known world. Their queries relate to business, marriage, politics, philosophy, all aspects of human endeavour. The answers – delivered, by preference, in hexameters – are frequently veiled: a man told he will die at the fall of a house spends the rest of his life out of doors, only to be killed when an eagle drops a tortoise on his head.

It is the end of the first century BC and the oracle at Delphi still exerts considerable influence, despite the rise and rise of Rome. Historically we find ourselves at a moment of shifting balance, a threshold straddled by the two great civilizations of the ancient world; as Rome ascends, Greece struggles to retain influence.

Readers familiar with the works of William Golding will feel immediately at home at such a threshold – think of *Lord of the Flies* teetering between civilization and anarchy, *The Spire* between earth and heaven, *Pincher Martin* between life and death. *The Double Tongue*, Golding's final work, was left unfinished when he died in 1993. By virtue of timing if nothing else, it occupies the most poignant threshold of the author's long and distinguished career.

Golding's publisher and literary executors chose to publish the first draft of *The Double Tongue* despite the existence of a complete second draft and the knowledge that Golding was about to embark upon a third. This initial draft was felt to be the fuller, truer realization of the author's vision and although it is quite possible to imagine further additions to the text, there is nothing of the literary fragment about it. It reads as a complete work, one of great delicacy and freshness.

The Double Tongue is Golding's only novel narrated in the voice of a woman. Like other Golding heroes, the Pythia, Arieka, is an outsider, wretchedly wrong-footed by her lack of social value (people whisper that she might better have been disposed of at birth), the fact that she is ugly, unmarriageable, unloved. When she catches the eye of the High Priest of Apollo, it is on account of her spiritual power, her naïveté and her nascent intelligence. Intrigued by rumours of half-miracles, and with an instinct for the girl's potential, the High Priest, Ionides, signs on as her guardian, accepts a dowry from the family and takes her to Delphi to serve the oracle.

At Delphi, he offers everything a downtrodden and deprived young woman might desire: vocation, friendship, freedom from social constraints and, quite wonderfully, a complete library of the world's books. Whether Arieka actually possesses the unique powers that justify such gifts remains unclear. There is the matter of a half-cooked fish restored to life and the healing of a sick baby, but Arieka's qualities appear to be mainly those of an unmarriageable girl as yet unredeemed by and unappreciated for her considerable subtlety of mind and strength of character. What she goes on to make of herself is a different story entirely, one that forms the centre of the novel.

The book opens with the eighty-year-old Arieka recounting her awkward, misfit girlhood; it is a coming-of-age tale in the classic, or perhaps classical, mould. Despite the huge gulf that initially separates her from her mentor, they grow together, united in occupation, familiarity, intellect and, most surprising of all, genuine tenderness. The High Priest's 'shuddering distaste for a woman's flesh' does not prevent them living together in a marriage of sorts, as Arieka says, 'I doubt if any married couple ever approaches [such] intimacy of thought and feeling.' As the relationship matures, a rare and satisfying partnership emerges.

Ionides' ambitions, however, reveal themselves to be political rather than spiritual, creating a minefield of hypocrisies and ambiguities for the fledgling Pythia. The High Priest says of Rome, 'That they will conquer the world is a nightmare that haunts me.' And when citizens of Rome (including Julius Caesar) travel to the oracle with enquiries about position and power, Ionides translates the god Apollo's pronouncements into answers expedient to his own agenda.

Within this commotion of ulterior motives, Arieka practises appeasement in equal measure with prophecy, managing over the course of her lifetime to carve out a place of integrity and peace. She and Ionides are as split on the subject of spirituality as any modern suburban couple – she believes in the gods, he doesn't – yet they meet in agreement at the value of Greek culture and the need to defend the oracle.

Notwithstanding its ancient setting, the novel is entirely modern in form, its characters and dialogue vivid and unconstrained (perhaps all writers should occasionally publish a first draft). *The Double Tongue* takes place over six decades in the life of the Pythia, yet seems to exist in a single soft moment at the last stand of beauty and intellect. In this, there are echoes of Golding's 1955 novel, *The Inheritors*, with its imagined moment of shift between Neanderthal and *Homo sapiens* civilizations. At Ionides' final confrontation with Rome, we feel some of the same helpless sorrow inspired by *The Inheritors'* Lok – as much as we root for Greece, or for Neanderthal, it is not to be.

Throughout, it is Arieka's quiet, unsentimental voice that guides the narrative, giving *The Double Tongue* its tone of gentle resolve. How irresistible to imagine Golding, towards the end of his life, speaking with his own double tongue – part Arieka, reconciling belief and duty, part Ionides, raging against the inexorable erosion of finer values, watching helplessly as life and empires wane, always with the regret, typical of old men, old women and old civilizations, that what lies ahead is worse than what has been.

In the end, it is as if the author, his priest and his Pythia stand together, reminiscing over long lives well-lived, contemplating what was lost, what was gained and what, if anything, mattered. Ionides' last gift to Arieka is the key to the door in the Pythia's deep cave, the door behind which we expect to find the cleft in the stone, the source of the oracle. What she discovers there is the book's final confirmation that the world is what we see, what we experience, and what we are able to imagine – nothing more.

It is as much a final statement as any author could desire.

I

Blazing light and warmth, undifferentiated and experiencing themselves. There! I've done it! The best I can, that is. Memory. A memory before memory? But there was no time, not even implied. So how could it be before or after, seeing that it was unlike anything else, separate, distinct, a one-off. No words, no time, not even I, ego, since as I tried to say, the warmth and blazing light was experiencing itself, if you see what I mean. Of course you do! It was a quality of, a kind of naked being without time or sight (despite the blazing light) and nothing preceded it and nothing came after. It is detached from succession, which means, I suppose, it may have happened at any point in my time – or out of it!

Where, then? I remember incontinence. My nurse and my mother – how young she must have been! – cried out with laughter which was also a reprimand. Could I speak before I could speak? How did I know there was the word 'reprimand'? Well, there is a whole bundle of knowledge we bring with us instantly; knowledge of what anger is, pain is, pleasure is, love. Either before or very closely after that incontinence there is a view of my legs and tummy in the warm sun. I am examining the modest slit between my legs experimentally with no knowledge of what it leads to, what it is for, nor that it defines me for the rest of my life. It is one of the reasons why I am here rather than in some other place. But I was unaware of Aetolia and Achaia and all the rest. There was more laughter, perhaps slightly furtive, and a reprimand. I am picked up and spanked very gently, no pain, only a sense of having done wrong.

Almost as far back is the time when I didn't have many words for myself and couldn't explain myself. Leptides, our neighbour's son, was kneeling by the great wall of our house and playing a game. He had a smouldering reed in one hand and a hollow reed in the other. He blew through the hollow reed and made a flame start off the end of the other. He looked just like one of our older house slaves who worked with copper and tin or silver and sometimes, but not often, with gold. I thought he might be making a tin ornament for me, which tells me that I started life as a hopeful child on the whole until I got to know about things. I squatted down to look. But he was burning up ants and doing it very neatly. He hit each one as a huntsman might and the ants were seldom scorched but completely burned up in an instant. I would have liked to have a go but knew that handling the two reeds at once would be beyond me. Besides, I had been taught not to play with fire! What interests me now is that I did not think of the ants as living things. My mind could go down as far as fish but no farther. Which is why the fish must come next.

We had a huge stone fish tank, so huge it had three grown-up steps to climb before you could see the fish in it. The time I'm thinking of must have been summer, for the water was low although the men kept bringing tubs of seawater up from the beach, but in my memory they never quite succeeded and the water stayed low until it got thoroughly rained on. Most of all I liked the time when the men brought fish up from our boats in barrels and sloshed them straight into the tank. How frisky the fish were then! They were frightened, I suppose, but they gave an appearance of joy and excitement. But they would soon calm down and seem contented and if not wanted immediately, stayed there, becoming kind of house fish and tame. They were easy to manage, like house slaves. I wonder was that the first time I compared one thing with another? This particular time Zoileus came to fetch them. He was a house slave, too, naturally. I am getting into a muddle. They were born slaves in our house, not caught in battle or raiding or punished for a crime or that sort of thing – say, being very poor for example. You know how it is. I was going to make another comparison and say it's like being born a girl, a woman, but that isn't so. There's a time in childhood when girls don't know how happy they are because they don't know they're girls if you see what I mean, though they find out later and most of them or some of them at any rate panic the way fish do in the pan. At least the lucky ones do. Anyway Zoileus simply dumped these fish in the oil which was smoking. One of the fish got its head over the edge of the pan and gaped its mouth at me.

I screamed. I went on screaming because it hurt so. I must have screamed things, not just screamed, for the next I remember is Zoileus shouting.

'All right! All right! I'll take them back –'

He stopped speaking then, for our house dame came quickly into the kitchen, the keys clanking at her waist.

'What on earth is the matter?'

But Zoileus had gone and the fish with him. My nurse explained that I had been frightened of the fish and maybe something should be offered up for luck, a root of garlic perhaps. Our house dame spoke kindly to me. Fish were made to be eaten and didn't feel things the way we free people did. She commanded Zoileus to bring back the pan and the fish. He explained that they were back in the tank.

'What do you mean, Zoileus, back in the tank?'

'They jumped out of the pan, lady, and swam off among the others.'

I have never known the truth of that. Fish fried in smoking oil can't swim away, there's no doubt of that. But Zoileus was not a liar. Perhaps he was, just this once. Perhaps he threw them away or hid them. Why? Well, supposing they did indeed swim away, it doesn't follow that I had anything to do with it. Still, people thought that was odd. The house slaves, good souls though ours were,

6

will believe anything and the more unlikely the better. We did all go solemnly to the tank but one fish is very like another and there was a whole shoal of them stacked in the shadow under the thatched half-roof. The house dame called my mother who called my father and by that time, whether his story was true or not, Zoileus had to stick to it. In the end, I think, he came to believe it himself, believed that some power had healed some half-burnt fish for no particular reason at all, which as far as my nurse was concerned was satisfyingly godlike. A bit of – not awe – but respect came my way too. In the end a sacrifice was made to the sea god, though in the case of a miraculous healing, Aesculapius or Hermes would surely have been more entitled. Had I been older at the time I might have thought it odd in view of my gender that they did not propitiate a goddess rather than a god. But which one? Neither Artemis nor Demeter nor Aphrodite would have had much use for me.

But I suppose I had better tell you something about us. We are Aetolians, naturally, since we live on the north side of the gulf. We were a Phocian family. My father is – was – a rich man and my oldest brother has inherited from him. Where our land touches the sea it stretches along for more than a mile. We have thousands of goats and sheep and a large old house with the usual dependencies and slaves and people. We also have a share in the sea ferry which sails across from the edge of our land to Corinth. Often the people who crossed used to think our house was

7

the next village higher up the valley and they would make their way to it after they had landed and expect a bed, or horses, or even a carriage. But a little while before I was born my honoured father had a notice put up where the ferry brought in the people. There was a wooden hand pointing up the valley past our land and letters on a board under the hand which said

TO DELPHI

So now the travellers don't bother us so much but go on up to the next village. Beyond that village and further, the oracle and the shrine and the college of priests hangs on the side of Parnassus. The oracle is a woman who is inspired by the god to say what is going to happen and so on. You'll know all about that whoever you are and wherever you live, all the world knows! A strong man can walk from our ferry up to Delphi in about half a day. I knew about the oracle when I was quite small, because we Phocians were responsible for guarding it. My grandfather Anticrates son of Anticrates took part in the appropriation. My honoured father (also called Anticrates) said that it was absolutely necessary. His father had told him when he was a small boy that it was necessary to take it under our protection. Delphi was inconceivably rich and it was quite obvious at the time that several cities (I name no names even now) were about to get their hands on all the treasure and waste it in impious ways. But, as he said, it was necessary to protect the place for we had a just war on our hands and the god agreed that we needed the gold for that purpose.

Living so near, being of such a degree and having taken part in it all, the family has many stories of what happened at the time. We used to keep some of our knowledge to ourselves but so many things have passed away I can tell you some of them now in my old age since they no longer matter. When we agreed with the Delphians and particularly with the college of priests to take them over we asked the Pythia – she was the oracle, of course you will remember that – we asked her to transmit to us the god's approval. But all she would do was cry 'Fire, fire, fire!' She came up the steps from the holy of holies into the portico and still cried 'Fire, fire, fire!' She ran wild and no one could do anything for her, the god had her in his hands, no one could touch her until at last she got among some ignorant soldiers – they were not Phocians but mercenaries – and they killed her!

It is quite true, said my father, that the oracle has never been the same since. He also said that there were a few fires in Delphi started by the mercenaries which was sufficient at the time to make her outcry quite understandable. But you can never really tell with an oracle. There are famous ones from earlier days. Once a man was told he would die by the fall of a house. So he stayed out of doors until one day an eagle dropped a tortoise on his bald head. The god speaks with a double tongue which he inherited

from a huge snake he killed at Delphi. As a matter of fact
– I have never told anyone of this – I myself have worked
out what was meant by the other fork of the tongue when
the Pythia cried out 'Fire, fire, fire!' For that year in which
we took over Delphi was also the year in which the God
Alexander the Great was born. You see, as all the world
knows, you can never tell with an oracle. But to say we
sacked the place is a monstrous lie. The war was very expensive and lasted a long time and if in the end the god
was not wholly on our side it does not need a theologian
to explain to us that such is his privilege.

However, don't run away with the idea that I am a wise
woman and have worked out everything. I am a muddled
person. Boys of our degree have been taught to think, or
think they have been taught to think, though all it generally
means is being able to catch you out and then shout 'Zany!
Zany!' But I am indeed muddled and have not made sense of
anything. I think I am muddled partly because I am a woman, partly because I was never taught to think and partly
because I am me. Why! These tablets I have written are full
of words and I haven't even told you my name! It is Arieka
and it is said to mean 'little barbarian'. When I was young
I would have liked to be called by a more resounding name,
Demetria, say, or Cassandra, or Euphrosyne. But I am stuck
with Arieka and there it is. Perhaps I looked like a little barbarian when I was born. Babies are so ugly.

After the fish my memories are successive so I don't
have any excuse for being muddled. But after the fish

things altered a little. My mother (not my nurse) took me aside and explained that I had drawn attention to myself. It felt a bit like when I was incontinent. The very words 'drawn attention to yourself' were a reprimand. I understood a little more of what a girl was.

Still, there was my dear brother Demetrios – on whom be blessings and good luck wherever he may be! He was my dearest possession. He taught me my letters. He was a few years older than I and had hair coming on his face. I still can't think why he did it and I dread the only explanation I can think of, which is that he was bored, but he drew shapes in the dust (imagine more sun!) and made me understand that each shape was uttering something. Then he put together two of those he had taught me and asked me what word they were saying and I was launched. It seems to me, remembering back, that I jumped from that first word clear over the hedges that some children find so hard and I read fluently from that moment. Of course this is impossible for two reasons. The first is that my brother only taught me a few letters on that first occasion and had to be pleaded with to 'play that game again!' The second reason is that I had no access to anything which would allow of fluent reading. There were very few books when I was a child. Of course there are more now, when people – and not the best people – have made a trade out of selling them. When I was a child, unless you had the luck to know a poet or writer well enough to beg his roll of paper off him, you had to put up with the tales people told at the hearth, the songs they sang, and if you were old enough to be present a story chanted to the whole assembled family by some wandering 'Son of Homer'.

Though the centre of the world is just a walk away up the hill from us, my brother was the only one who had a book. It was his schoolbook and told the story of Odysseus in only a very few columns. He shared a schoolmaster with our neighbour's son, but when he was sixteen – my brother I mean – he went off to Sicily to look after things there like sending corn in ships and so on and trading. As he left, laughing and shouting, he tossed the book to me and said, 'Read that to me when I come back!' The sorrows of childhood are complete and for many days I did not bother to examine the book, but at last I did and perhaps my sorrow was not as complete as I had thought, for when Demetrios came back after six months I could indeed read the book. But Demetrios was very manly, almost unrecognizable, and he had forgotten me, let alone his book. Then, after ten days or so, he went away again. Still, I could read and knew the book by heart. The result was that when a 'Son of Homer' was invited into the women's part of the house and gave us a section of the *Odyssey* – as I remember, the very famous bit when he's in Phaeacia – the man said (bowing to my mother) that now he had seen our house he understood that Odysseus did not immediately speak out, because he was awed at the magnificence of the palace of Alcinous. After the man had finished, I was exalted and cried out that he should go on to tell us how Odysseus had met Athene on the beach: but that exaltation led to me being told that I had drawn attention to myself again. I remember how envious I was of the boy who carried the man's lyre and had seen so much of the world. I had a daydream of disguising myself as a boy and going off with the man, though I never found a satisfactory way of getting rid of his boy, who was always there at the back of my daydream to bring me down to earth and back to my senses.

I learnt about love and grief when my brother Demetrios went away for the second time. I don't know whether I was a scrawny little girl before he went away but I am very sure I was soon afterwards. My face has always been uneven, the one side not properly balanced by the other. Generally people say that girls of my kind are redeemed by animation or a pair of beautiful eyes, but I wasn't. Leptides, the son and heir of the smaller estate which marched with ours, was just as scrawny, but seeing that he was a boy it didn't matter. He had light sandy hair and light brown freckles all over his pink face. He called himself a 'light-haired Achaian' as in the war story. He and his two sisters were allowed to play with me but that all came to a sudden end. Leptides used to make up games in which I and his sisters were his army and sometimes his wives or his slaves. His army was Alexander's, of course, and far more strictly disciplined than the Macedonians ever were as far as I've heard.

My nurse was supposed to be supervising these games, but she was getting fat and foolish and slept most of her life away, a natural slave and only worth punishing for the look of the thing. One day when I was his slave, he said that since I was no longer a free woman I should be beaten on my bare bottom. Of course in real life, and particularly in a great house like ours, the house slaves are never beaten. They are more or less adopted into the family, at least the girls are. It hurt a great deal though I didn't mind it as much as you might think. Looking back I believe Leptides was jealous of our house and estate. That makes sense, but of course it's the kind of insight you only get when you are much older; or perhaps you know it when you are young but don't know it – there you go, Arieka, getting things muddled again! But you can see how ignorant or innocent a child I was in that I asked my nurse whether a house slave could really be beaten on her bare bottom or whether she would be allowed to draw her himation tightly over her bottom. I was not prepared for the following questions nor the commotion my answers started. Nurse had palpitations and hot flushes and breathlessness. How she summoned up courage enough to tell my mother what was going on I cannot think. Not only was I forbidden to play with Leptides any more but I had some more bread and water and hemming to teach me something or other.

When I came out again I had to stand in front of my honoured father with my hands properly clasped in front and my eyes looking at the floor midway between us. My mother started to speak but my father silenced her with a gesture.

'In this kind of situation, Demetria, it is almost always the girl's fault.'

There was a long silence after that. My father broke it at last.

'I suppose you know, young lady, that you've got young Leptides into trouble? He's been sent off to do three months' military training. I don't wish to see you any more. Now go.'

So I curtsied and went to my place. Of course, whatever my father said, the military training was not really a punishment like bread and water, solitude and plain hemming. My mother said it would get all the nasty thoughts out of his head and he might even form a lasting friendship with one of our brave soldiers. Of course the men of our degree are cavalry. Indeed, boys who get sent early to military training think it's a holiday and come back boasting of being on watch in the middle of the night 'like the other men'. I was very lonely at this time and became acutely aware of my own insignificance. In addition to being scrawny with a lopsided face I am on the sallow side. My nurse told me that my father would have to pay an extra large dowry to get me off his hands, which is why he was so stern with me. She said it was enough to make any man stern because what did he get out of it? The proper dowry for a girl of my degree – provincial aristocrat – would be a thousand silver pieces. He would have to pay more like two thousand.

There were times, as I moved towards my courses,

when I still had hopes that the gods and in particular Aphrodite would work their customary miracle and turn a child with my natural disadvantages into a flower-like creature and do it more or less in a single night. There is a dread insult in our part of the world, and I sometimes thought I saw it behind the faces of the people responsible for me – the thought that I should have been disposed of at birth, though of course no one ever uttered the words and I dare not myself. But the thought was there, behind their faces.

I was brooding on all this one day and going towards the fish tank when one of our boughten slaves came whining out of their place with a child in her arms and thrust it at me. She was howling by the time she reached me. My arms came up automatically to cradle, but almost as quickly I used them to push the child back at her for it was covered with spots. She, curious creature, fell silent at that, ducked a lame reverence and walked back again into her own place. But I had felt something in the instant between holding and letting go. I should be hard put to describe it further. So my simplest recourse is to tell you baldly that the girl believed I had some power and that once I had touched the child it would get better, which it did. This goes back to the half-cooked fish, a story which was now a bit of family history and, like most family history, simplified and exaggerated. I do not think I am a healer and I am the one to know, surely!

We are wrapped in mysteries. I know that. I have come

to know that. Until I had my courses time did really stand still for me. I know that too. Yet among us Hellenes, whether we are Aetolians or Achaians or no matter what, courses come later according to our degree. I was in my fifteenth year. Things made a kind of unruly sense. This time it wasn't fish or even a baby, but a donkey. I have told nobody, ever. This donkey turned the mill for the coarse grain. Naturally, meal for the family was done at a rotary quern with the slave women singing the turning song, usually the one about Pittacus, but quite often if another name would fit the turning they used it. This donkey, which naturally again we all called Pittacus, walked round and round and at the end of a bar a huge ball of stone rolled round in a groove full of grain, or sometimes the mush from the olive's third pressing. Well of course you know how that kind of mill works! I was watching Pittacus and interested in his thing which he had under his belly which was sticking out and hurting him because he was braying so loudly as he walked round. This thing was as if alive on its own and quite separate from poor Pittacus it seemed. Every now and then it would snap up against his belly with a sound like hitting a big drum. It was then that a weirdness overcame me so that I felt I might fall down. But I pushed through that because I was interested and horrified and frightened. At the moment when I emerged – if emerged is the right word – one of our boughten slaves came with a gag and I was fascinated by the struggle. He had to strap the animal's jaws

17

together to keep its mind on the work in hand. Pittacus was trying to rear, but could do nothing but strike out sideways with a hind leg. I found out afterwards that he had scented one of our most valued mares which was to mate with my father's war stallion, so Pittacus couldn't be let go even when the mush was all pulped.

There is something very strange about girls immediately before menstruation. I don't mean the pretty ones, the beauties or even those who are comely enough to be welcomed into a family with only a modest dowry. I mean really the unattractive ones, whom a god has blighted and who have nothing for sale and who have become so defensive they can never make contact with anyone, least of all with the rites of the Paphian. They acquire, these unfortunates, strange abilities. Or perhaps abilities is the wrong word. The situation is not really describable, except that the girl becomes very clever in a useless way – useless it may be to anyone else, though the girl may think there is substance in it. Well. It may be indescribable but I will do my best. It is a furtive power. They wish: and if they wish in the right way – wrong way? – sometimes, if the balance is ever so slightly on their side, then – just more often than not but only just – they get what they want or somebody does. The world is riddled with coincidences and the girl sees this. She uses this when it is available. Perhaps to somebody else who gets what he wants. Or, I mean, gets what he didn't want. You can never prove this. As I said it is furtive and dishonest, knows

18

how to hide, how to claim, how to disguise, avoid, speak double like the snake or not at all. Moreover, this is not a power to be exaggerated. It is no oracle, does not win battles. It cannot cure the plague but only some head-aches, cannot cure heartache but can supply the necessary tears for it.

When my father clapped me up on bread and water the first time, he took my doll away. I wished it back but, of course, how could it come? But when they let me out I knew where they had put it and went straight there. I knew indeed where it was, went and took it because they were such and such and would put it there. So I watched the donkey Pittacus struggling against the spikes in his gag and the weirdness overcame me and I quietened him, feeling the consolation and love go out, out through my aching head and suddenly reeling mind, out to poor Pittacus, and quietened him in his struggle so that his tail dropped and his member drew back in and he stood silent at the mill with his head down by his feet. It was at that moment that I heard a shout of laughter and there was Leptides grinning over the wall of the yard and showing his teeth through a sandy beard and crying aloud to the whole world: 'He fancies you!' Into that blazing moment, drawn and irritated by the ass's clamour, strode my father. He stopped ten yards away. He went white, turned and fairly ran into the house. My head cleared as if he had run out of it. There was a great silence of change and discovery. I heard a faint but positive *tap* and, by some instinct looking down, I saw the first drop of my blood starred on the strap of my right sandal.

After that of course I disappeared into the women's quarters and the usual sacrifices were made. I went into a five-day period of seclusion. The ass in rut and Leptides' loud, male laughter and his shouting out what ought not be said – they were a kind of initiation into my new state.

I must have been happy some of the time. I think girls are created to be happy for a time in childhood. They can be happier in their skins than men, or boys rather, who have always to be doing something, mischief probably. But now of course, aged fifteen, I was grown up. It was difficult. Sometimes I think, and indeed thought at this early experience of being grown up, that we should be free and natural as birds are. What should we think of a bird which was different and feverish, that never flew but sat all the time on a nest? But my parents expected such normality. It should have been easy enough, for all I had to worry about were my courses and all the rituals attached, but the rituals didn't bother me and my courses hardly hurt me – merely added to the confusion in my head and a slight headache for a day and a half. They were just enough to remind me that women aren't free, not even the free ones. It was like a not very heavy chain which had been waiting to fasten itself round my waist to ensure that I was a prisoner like all women. The only consolation was that for a few days each month I was untouchable. What followed was that on those days I could have any thoughts I wanted without the gods taking any notice of them, because the thoughts were untouchable, too. I have never told anyone this truth because it is a mystery and only to be written down rather than spoken. So on those days when I was thought to be unclean I found myself thinking all kinds of forbidden thoughts and planning to put them away somewhere safe. I do it now for I am in my eighties and what does anything I do matter?

As I was grown up, when my father had guests who were suitable – and I don't think my father ever had guests who weren't – I was sometimes allowed to sit on a high chair by my mother in hers. Of course neither my mother nor I said anything on these occasions and if a guest was so forgetful of his manners as to address either of us directly my father would answer for us as was proper. So, though I saw Ionides very soon after I grew up, I never spoke to him. He was rangy and restless and gaunt. Though he was not much more than thirty years old there was grey in his hair and a grey tone round his mouth and chin where he had shaved in the Alexandrian manner. He smiled sometimes out of his gaunt face and you could see how the muscles moved under the skin. It was a strange smile. There was a grief in its appearance which I am sure enough he did not really feel. It was there, you might say, partly by accident and partly by his position which was distinguished. He was, in fact, the priest who had to interpret the mouthings of the Pythia when she was beside herself on account of inspiration. The second visit he made, there came a moment when he actually smiled at me, which in a younger and less distinguished man would have been suggestive. But it was a kind, sad smile and it moved me much as my brother had done. I dared to smile downward slightly and drew my scarf closer. I was conscious of wearing my best dress, the one with the egg and dart border. I am sure there was some kind of communication he intended, after an appraisal taken. It was like the first glint of the sun. The very next day my father sent for me. This was not to the large hall where we entertained our guests but to a smaller room, the estate office in fact, where there was the only paper in the house and large bundles of tally sticks. My father was flicking the balls of his abacus. As I came in, he threw the tablets at an estate slave who waited before him.

'Add them up for yourself!'

When the slave had gone my father turned to me.

'You may sit down there.'

I got up on the three-legged stool which was slightly too high for me and waited. He opened a box and took out a document which I could see was written on all over and beautifully written at that. He unrolled it and muttered the contents to himself.

'So and so the son of so and so, blah blah, has given for partnership of marriage, blah, her mother being blah to blah son of blah. Bride brings so much –'

'But, Honoured Father –'

'Don't interrupt. This is a great day for you, young lady. Where was I? "Son of blah, bride brings – let husband and wife live together – duties of marriage – if separation – let the husband restore – father of the husband Leptides – contract valid written in duplicate – each party – "'

'Father!'

'Don't interrupt – "and in answer to the formal question – "'

'I won't! I won't marry him! Who does he think he is?'

'Leptides son of Leptides. You must have known.'

I found I had climbed down from the stool. I was twisting my hands one with the other. I suppose it's what they call wringing.

'What does he want?'

My father snorted.

'He wants to finish the job if I remember rightly.'

'Never! Never!'

'Now listen, my girl –'

And still wringing my hands I did listen, and heard all the arguments which might be expected. My parents knew best. Leptides was a fine young man – well, not too bad a young man – I would thank them when I showed them their grandchild. Considering the dowry I had to bring him I ought to be down on my knees begging for forgiveness from my parents who had done more than their best for me. Who did I think I was? The Queen of Egypt? Get up, child, it's not as bad as all that. Women must be married or where should we be? It's ordained by the gods and who was I and so on . . .

Who was I indeed? I was already down on my knees but it was not in supplication. It was in panic and anguish through which I actually heard the threat of more bread and water and was ordered angrily to go back to my room and think about it. I did that, scurrying away like a mouse in a rickyard – not even a rat. When I got back to my room I walked up and down, up and down, arms crossed on my bosom, hands beating the upper arm, what they call with women beating your breast though not even the deepest grief or terror would make a woman do that, up and down, up and down. I went mad, I think. Crouched on my pallet bed I saw there was only one thing for it. I must escape somehow. I must get away – but where? I thought of my brother and determined that I must go in his direction – towards Sicily – something would happen, the gods would protect me.

Now, at my age, I know a strange thing. I was going through the motions of escape. What I was doing was making a last utterly desperate appeal to my parents: see! I am even willing to face death to escape this fate! But at the same time the underside of my mind knew it was an appeal. The only honest determination of my mind was this: I will go towards Sicily and I will go *as far as I can.*

I will not elaborate on the contrivances I made. It involved getting the boughten slave who thought she owed her son's life to me to get me a boy's tunic. The necessary companion of this foolish escapade – foolish if I did not admit it was an appeal, but sensible otherwise − was, of all creatures, Pittacus. The only people who saw us leave by way of the back court were slaves who were at once astonished and frightened. I was astride the ass in my tunic with a scarf draped over my legs and Pittacus did not much like my weight where it was, as a change from the mill to which he was so accustomed as to think it the only way of living. He had also, what was very natural, a tendency to turn in a circle if I was not keeping him straight, which I could only do by whacking on the turning hand with a stick. We had got no more than a hundred yards along the track above the beach when I heard the horn from the hill. The next thing I heard was a great belling of hounds and shouts of men, which confounded Pittacus who wanted to go back home. I had got him pointed towards Sicily when the clamour increased suddenly. A full-grown stag came round the corner of the path with three hounds hanging from him and the rest of the pack boiling round him and the men on horses only a few yards behind. Even at that moment I did not understand my peril and felt for the poor stag and its terror so that it turned aside and dragged the snarling hounds down the beach towards the water. The hounds had a go at Pittacus and when he felt a real bite he bucked hugely and threw me into the air. I fell on a hound or two which broke my fall but it was still heavy enough to knock me out.

I came to, to feel my tunic tearing. Leptides and Ionides were either side of me, keeping the horses' hoofs clear of me and whipping the hounds away. The anger and contempt in their eyes – and the laughter in the faces of the riders who now crowded round – were worse than the nips I had suffered from the hounds. I find it hard to believe at this distance of time, but it was indeed Leptides who chased the stag into the water and ordered the huntsman to cut its throat while Ionides wrapped his cloak and my scarf about me and set me before him on his horse. I did notice even then how he winced at the touch of my flesh and how, when he saw what I tried so desperately to conceal from him, his face twisted in disgust. But I was ignorant, weeping and sore. I had made my appeal sure enough and now had to abide the consequences of it. I passed the next few hours in a kind of deliberate insensibility. They took me back to the house, called for my mother, said things, everybody said things. At one point Leptides was whipping off our boughten slaves, the house slaves had too much sense to interfere. At last I was in my own room, wearing a dress just like a grown woman, my nips smarting where they had laid salve on them, my mother standing by the window and closing the shutters as if there had been a dead body in the room. I wished at the time that there had been. When they were closed and the room in an artificial twilight she still stood looking down at me.

'You fool.'

After that, there was a long pause. She began to walk up and down, then stopped again.

'What are we to do with you?'

Still I drew myself in and hid in my own mind.

Presently my mother left me. There is not much to say about my state except that it is a retreat, further and further away from the daily world. It is not a drawing into one's self; or rather it is, I suppose, since in those circumstances where else is there to go? But what it feels like is a deliberate descent into the earth, down and down. Each time I realized afresh the enormity of my disgrace, the depth of my shame, I drew myself in and thrust myself down, down, away from the daylight, away from people. Also away from the gods. I suppose that was where my ignorant but now one-pointed mind came on a fact which would have astonished me if I had been in a condition to think round it. The fact was that I missed the gods and was not just ashamed, but stricken down with grief, and when at last I got to the level where there were no people but only gods, my heart broke. Do not think it was this god or that. They had drawn together in a sacred band. Even our herm, the cheeky column with the privates of a man and a bearded face, who stood, fronting the path from the ferry, even he seemed glad in my imagination to be turned away from me.

Oh, that child! It is a kind of self-love I suppose that makes me smile to myself when I remember her. Well. For all the ascetics say, a degree of self-love is no bad thing. It makes life possible, unless like the ascetics you think it wholly bad and to be rid of as soon as you can.

But whatever you think of her, whatever I remember of her there is no doubt about the poor thing's shame and grief with her gods turning their back on her! Until then I had accepted them as being there because everyone else – grown-ups I would say – believed in them or said they did. I was too young and ignorant to know that people do not always believe what they say they do. Anyway, in that small room, with its pallet, its single chest, its hooks with one or two cloaks hanging from them, there in the artificial twilight she dropped down into grief, into sorrow beyond the shame. She dissolved away like a lump of salt in fresh water. There was nothing but grief before the retreating backs of the gods: then they were gone.

There is a void when the gods have been there, then turned their backs and gone. Before this void as before an altar there is nothing but grief contemplating the void. Time passes but irrelevantly. The void with the grief before it is eternal. Even the sound of the wooden bolt being shot back and the latch lifting did not alter that contemplation. My mother's voice was more deeply bitter than I had ever heard before.

'He has withdrawn his offer. Leptides, that oaf, has withdrawn his offer. He' – and it sounded as if she spat the words out – 'He pities us!'

Life is not bad. It is intolerable, which is different. I sat up heavily. I stared at my mother's feet.

'He doesn't want the thousand pieces of silver?'

'What decent man would when a woman went with it

28

who has shown everything she's got to half Aetolia? But a boy, heir to no more than a farm, to turn down alliance with us – with us!'

I heard the door close again and the latch drop. I listened for the wooden bolt to move but it never did. Well. What bolt is needed to cage a naked girl?

Presently I sat up, then stood up. I felt my nips and they had hardly broken the skin. The hounds were well enough trained – no Molossian dogs those! They had known their place and the difference between human skin and a stag's leather. I took my phial of olive oil and rubbed a little of it into my face. I thought to myself that if Leptides had gone through with his offer I might have asked him for a mirror – and flinched at once from the bloodless image of his voice: *What would you want with a mirror?* I combed my hair out but unravelled the knots with my fingers. I had neither so much hair nor so many combs that I could afford to lose any of them. I eyed my open chest with its folded clothes. The best one lay on top. I moved it on to my pallet and took out a dark gown that had frayed round the hem at the heel. I put it on slowly then fastened it with bronze brooches on either shoulder. I girdled myself and crossed the straps between my small, not to say insignificant breasts, then pulled up the skirt to let it hang down over the girdle.

You will wonder why I did all this, I who had been grief before the void, but the reason is simple. Nature has a world of imperatives and I needed to obey one of them.

It is odd how people in stories never need to ease themselves, and that bitch Helen never menstruated – no, no, not bitch – poor soul! So I went out through the unbolted door and into the privy and eased myself, thinking now I was no longer before it that of course the void was the door of death, which explained everything and brought me a measure of peace: for I saw that death was an escape and a refuge. That is a hard lesson for the young to understand unless they have really been brought before the void by the unbearable cruelty of life itself! The others are right to dance and sing and have best friends and marry a good man and love their children. When I was back in my room I wondered what to do next, which shows that I was properly alive again and even a bit hungry. But before I had come to any conclusion my mother opened the door and came in quickly.

'Arieka! No, not that dress, your best one quickly!'

'To wear?'

'Quickly, I said! For Heaven's sake get that old thing off and put on your egg and dart! You can wear the gold earrings today and the bracelet. Hurry!'

'What is it, Mother?'

'Hurry, I said! I want you looking your best.'

'Oh, not Leptides! I won't –'

'No. Not Leptides. Forget him and hurry. Your father wants you.'

After I had changed as fast as I could – and my mother fussed round, pushing a strand of hair this way, pulling up

30

the skirt, muttering and blessing herself – we went, she in front, of course, I following with hands folded at my waist. But they came up of themselves.

He was not alone. He lay on one couch and Ionides on the other. Ionides gave me his slight version of the smile with its accompanying sorrow. My father opened the proceedings.

'You may sit, Demetria.'

Ionides stirred.

'And the girl, old friend? The girl too, don't you think?'

My father pointed to the other chair. I got myself on to it rather clumsily if the truth were to be told. My fear seemed to swirl round me. My father cleared his throat.

'Ionides Peisistratides has with great generosity offered us a way out of our – what shall I call them?'

'Your difficulties,' murmured Ionides, 'your temporary difficulties. Or do I sound too much like a money-lender?'

'Our difficulties,' said my father. 'Precisely. He has made us an offer on your behalf. He proposes to nominate you as a ward of the Foundation.'

There was a silence. My father stared at me, then at my mother, then at Ionides, then back at me.

'Can't you say something?'

But I was not used to saying something. There was, as I think the saying goes, an ox on my tongue. It was Ionides who answered him at last.

'I think, old friend, that you had better leave this to me.'

He heaved himself up on the couch, turned a little,

31

swung his legs and put his feet on the floor. He was sitting on the edge of the couch, just as if he had been a girl! I shall never forget that moment. I might have laughed but did not. But it was, to say the least, odd to face a man sitting opposite me. It was certainly odd, but easier.

'What has happened, Arieka, is that after all the excitement – I mean after the – well, you are called a little barbarian aren't you, so may I use a barbarian word I picked up on my travels and say that after the *shemozzle* this morning your parents find themselves, think themselves in a fix. Now you've decided to refuse that young man and, believe me, I agree with you, the way is open for me to propose what I was going to before I heard you were contemplating matrimony. You see, I'm really a rather important person –'

My father laughed.

'A very important person.'

'If you say so, old friend. Very well. At least an important person in that I can decide a girl is suitable for the service of the shrine at Delphi.'

'Don't get the wrong idea,' my father broke in. 'You'll sweep floors.'

'That is putting a rather dreary construction on the offer, don't you think? You see, my dear, there is a college of priests at Delphi. The Foundation, that is the divinely constituted body which actually runs the place, if you see what I mean, also has to decide what persons are worthy of belonging to the service of the god in however slight

32

and menial a position. You have heard of the Pythia of course? Or I should say in fact the Pythias. At the moment there are two of them. Those distinguished ladies are sacred and divine and utter the oracles of the god' – my parents and Ionides himself made a sacred sign – 'but we are not directly concerned with them. After all' – and he smiled again – 'we have slaves to do what I may call "the dirty work"!'

'You must think yourself lucky, my girl,' said my father. 'Don't imagine you're not costing us anything!'

'The Foundation,' murmured Ionides, 'is not a charitable institution. It must, if I may so phrase it, *pay its way*. Your father, Anticrates the son of Anticrates, and I have come to an agreement on behalf of your family and the Foundation. Your dowry will be held by the Foundation. On your death – we have to mention such things, my dear, when discussing legal matters – on your death it would become Foundation property in perpetuity. Should you wish to marry at any point the Foundation would return the whole sum to you but keep the interest.'

'Ion, old friend, we should mention the sum to her don't you think?'

'I am sure a young lady like Arieka would not be interested in such sordid details. I should say, Arieka – now I really think you should uncross your arms, you know! That's better. You see, what your being a ward of the Foundation really comes to is that I have adopted you and shall be responsible for you. Do you mind that? Could you possibly bear it do you think? I should have to be responsible for your education in your duties and – oh heavens – a whole host of things. I hope we shall be friends.'

Beside me I heard my mother stir. I also heard in her voice that she had come to boiling point for she fairly hissed the words, 'Say something!'

But the words which came out of my mouth were nothing but astonishment.

'W-why me?'

My father answered the question instantly and grimly.

'Because we've paid an arm and a leg to get –'

'Old friend! I think we have all said very nearly enough. The question now is how soon can the girl pack up and come? She has a maid, I suppose? You'll send her up in a proper vehicle? We have to think of the reputation of the Foundation, you know! To answer your question, Arieka, we think, after what we have heard, that there may be qualities lying dormant – I mean asleep – in you which are – dare I say? – unusual; oh, nothing to be proud of, I assure you, but qualities in which we – well there. Everything will explain itself.'

'Where will she live?'

'Oh, we have the appropriate accommodation, old friend. It's a large foundation, you know, all those souls! And as I happen to be the Warden –'

'She can think herself lucky,' said my father shortly. 'Is there anything else?'

'We'll nominate our man for the agreement and you'll

nominate yours, I suppose. But she can come before that. We have no differences do we? Everything is straight and plain.'

'We don't want the girl any more.'

'I hope you mean that as far as she is concerned the affair is settled to her satisfaction? Any other meaning –'

My mother stood up, so I did too. She spoke, 'Ionides Peisistratides, I thank you.'

My father favoured me with a glare.

'Well, girl? Aren't you going to say anything?'

'Honoured Father.'

'To Ionides I mean.'

But again my words were the wrong ones and made little sense.

'This wonderful day –'

The last I saw of Ionides that time he was not smiling but laughing out loud, a thing he seldom did.

My mother fairly pushed me out.

II

The last winter snow on the broad head of Parnassus; somewhere there in the deep valleys at the knee of the mountain was Delphi, the centre of the earth.

I was woken out of an uneasy sleep at dawn. I had dreamed confusedly and in those days took much account of dreams, though mostly I dismiss them now. Every day we rid ourselves of the rubbish of our bodies. I think that in sleep with its dreams we are trying to rid ourselves of the rubbish of our minds. Not of course that I would have had such precise thoughts in those days. I was merely aware, with a faint feeling of distaste, that the people who ordered their actions by the dreams they had were trying to walk on water. That day began as usual, at first light. I was no sooner dressed and wrapped in an overmantel than my father summoned me before him. When I had curtsied with both hands hidden, he took up a small washleather bag and handed it to me. As I took it my hand touched his and I whipped it back. He said, in what for him was a kindly voice, that it did not matter.

'Your mother has told me that you are purified. You may kiss my hand.'

I did so with another curtsy.

'Open the bag.'

It will come as a surprise to those of a later generation – or perhaps to those of our own generation but below our degree – that I did not know what the things were. They were round and golden and had the head of the God Alexander the Great on them. I could not see any pins or catches for wearing them.

'Have you nothing to say?'

'Honoured Father, what are they?'

There was a pause. Then he gave a great shout of laughter.

'At least nobody can say you have not been well brought up! Well. Keep them close. "Honoured Father, what are they?" Did you know the story of the young wife who did not complain of her husband's stinking breath because she thought all men were like that? Menander would make a play out of it. Well you must go along now. Ask Ion what they are. He'll tell you – and dine out on the story!'

He waved me away and went back to his accounts. At least I knew what *they* were.

'Thank you, Honoured Father. Goodbye.'

I waited for him to say something, but all he did was grunt and wave me away again. My mother was waiting for me.

'Everything is ready. Come.'

Our brake was ready. There was a wain with my boxes in it and Chloe looking far too pretty and with far too much of her face uncovered but I said nothing. I wondered busily, in a mean little mind, if Ionides would allow me to sell her. But he was there, waiting, his groom holding the horse ready. Presently my mother laid one hand on my shoulder, drew aside my scarf and kissed me on the cheek.

'Be a good girl if you can. People will forget in time. The blessing of all the gods go with you.'

That did, at last, make me cry. Crying, I was lifted by Ionides into the brake, crying I heard the orders, saw the group of horsemen turn towards the gate. It was a considerable procession for a floor-sweeper. But then, Ionides was an important man. We passed into the outer courtyard, passed through the Great Gate.

'Stop! Stop! O please! Stop!'

I stumbled from the brake, snatched my skirts out of the dust and ran to him, stooped and flung my arms round him. It was our old herm, of course, standing deep in the earth with his privates jauntily displayed and his cheeky smile. I flung my arms round him and pressed my cheek to the stony curls of his head. I hated our house and would have left a curse on it if I had dared. But this was our old herm, that had been dug up after his permission had been sought and granted, dug up all those years ago by our little house in Phocis which he had guarded for so long. And now I was being dug up, torn up, transplanted without anyone asking my permission. I howled there as the sun rose on my future and I clung absurdly to my unhappy past.

'I think I had better share your brake with you. Come, little Arieka. You have wept enough as is seemly and any more would be a sheer indulgence. You don't seem like an indulgent girl to me. Come along. Now if you hold on there with your right hand – so – then put your left foot there – and lift up – good. Now sit down. He is a fine horse is he not? My hunter! But we will let my groom lead him. You know, since I am your guardian and you are my ward it would be quite appropriate for you to uncover more of your face – on the other hand the dust that is kicked up by this antiquated vehicle – you don't really know much about me or this journey do you?'

I said nothing for I did not know how to speak to a man. But he divined my difficulty.

'Now what are you to call me? If it comes to that, what am I to call you? Shall we settle for Arieka mostly, and Young Lady on high days and feast days? I think that's about right. As for what you call me, I think "Ion" would present you with a difficulty whereas "Ionides" with "Peisistratides" attached would do for those occasions in Delphi which are so fearfully solemn.'

'Yes, Honoured Ionides.'

'You are exquisitely well-mannered my child. Do you think I could be allowed to see both eyes instead of just one? It's difficult getting used to men. You have my entire sympathy. I prefer women. But don't tell anybody. I don't mean I prefer women as wives or slaves – that slave of yours is far too pretty, we must sell her – no, I mean women as friends. So, from my point of view, I am delighted to have made a new woman friend and be given the privilege of looking after her. You may notice that I talk too much. You, very properly, talk too little – a paradox! You are watching the apple going up and down in my throat. It is indeed prominent. We lanky creatures suffer from that sort of exposure. I daresay you could draw the muscles of my face. Well. You seem a little more comfortable, a walking pace. Your father keeps good cattle. But I should not be talking about that! Are you curious about your own future?'

'My mother told me I was to sweep floors, Honoured Ionides.'

He smiled with sorrow lurking round his eyes.

'I may have given her that impression. How foolish of me! Oh, now I understand. Yes. You will indeed carry the sacred besom in one of the processions. But otherwise –'

'I wouldn't have to go near *that* place?'

'Now what are you thinking of? What on earth – Yes, I see. I might have known you would be profoundly religious. Of course.'

'I'm not, I'm not! I'm . . . frightened. That's all.'

'It's much the same thing in the long run. Forgive me, I didn't mean to say that and you must forget it. My sense of the dramatic makes off with me. Anything for a point, a squib, a paradox, a neat apothegm – What is truth? But you believe in the gods?'

43

'Of course, Ionides.'

'It is good.'

'They are there, aren't they? You do believe they are, even without being frightened?'

'I believe it is entirely right for you to believe in them, poor babe. Never let go of them. Who knows –?'

There was a shout from some man or other and our procession ground and clopped to a halt. Men dismounted and hurried into the thorn bushes by the road. Ionides got down and went too. I had watched the floor of the vehicle or Ionides' face. Now I lifted my eyes to the view and cried out. The whole of the deep blue gulf lay before me, and far away the great central mountains of the Peloponnesus lifted their snowy heads into the sky. Just across the gulf, yet seeming near enough to touch, was the glitter and smoke of Corinth with the fortress of Acrocorinth. I had not known that the world could look like this and I could have gazed at it for ever.

But the men had done their business and were returning. Ionides jumped up into the brake and nodded to the leader of the armed men. The leader gave a shout and dust began to rise again as we ground on up the road.

'Honoured Ionides –'

'Yes?'

'The sacred besom.'

'The god has his household too, you know – his cook, his bodyservant, his sweeper. You wouldn't expect a god to do his own sweeping would you? But it's entirely symbolic. His bodyservant shakes a few grains of gold dust out of a shoe and you wave the sacred besom over it seven times. I think it is seven times. On these occasions it is usually either three or seven and just now and then, nine. The gods can count, you see.'

'I suppose so.'

'I think you are feeling braver already.'

'Look at all that, that world!'

'I do, often.'

'And our forest down there, and the pastures – Oh, Aetolia is beautiful!'

'I am not an Aetolian myself, but yes, Aetolia is beautiful. By the way, I am an Athenian. You have heard of Athens?'

'That is where the barbarians were beaten.'

'Yes. A long time ago. Since then – Athens would be over there on our left, way beyond those hills, more or less in a line with Megara.'

'That's Corinth across there. Sicily would be on our right wouldn't it?'

'My goodness, you do know a lot. Yes. Sicily would be on our right and a bit south and also a long, long way away.'

We were silent for a time. I thought of my brother but said nothing about him. What was there to be said? Ionides broke the silence at last.

'Now what are you wondering?'

'The future. My future. All the questions. Where? How? What?'

45

'As you probably remember there are two Pythias. One, the reigning Pythia, is a very distinguished lady indeed. She is blind but only to this world from which we are travelling backwards. The other is a younger lady. She is not . . . not such as the blind Lady. But the god permits himself to speak through whom he will. There is no merit in being an oracle, a Pythia. They are as they are, the reigning Lady is ancient, distinguished and, I would say, holy. The younger one is as you will find, for – symbolically – you will be her servant. Of course, we have slaves to do the actual work. Not that pert creature of yours, slaves born to the Foundation. Really, I sometimes think they know more about it than we do! Each of the gods, of the many, many gods, has his priest, his servant. Together they make up all souls and I am their Warden, or did I tell you that? Probably. It is my only claim to fame though. You are a good listener, my dear, and bring the worst out in me, I mean the most loquacious. You will live in your own apartment in what we call the palace of the Pythias. You will have your own servants. I shall teach you the duties and the methods of the position which I hope one day you will hold.'

'What is that, Ionides?'

'You will learn to listen and to speak the very words of the god.'

It was as if the world had fallen on me.

'God help me! No! Ionides –'

He raised his voice.

'It is a matter of some half-burnt fish and a child that recovered at the door of death.'

'Ionides, please! It was a mistake – people made it bigger –'

'Yes. Of course it was a mistake. Two mistakes. But you are exactly right. You are' – and he gave a curious kind of wincing shrug – 'a virgin. And you have . . . what you have. You are ignorant, and ignorance such as yours makes you look like a seer.'

'But for what? For what?'

'Look out there, all that. Achaia on one side of the gulf, Aetolia here. That was Sparta and Argos. Over there, shining Athens, Thebes, the Islands – so many names, so much history – but Athens is a village. She is full of fake men holding fake offices. Aetolia – a string of farms – and Delphi – Delphi to which kings sent their embassies, and Alexander begged to come – Socrates – oh, child! I will tell you! See, over there to our right, yes, is Sicily. But also, far nearer, is an awful future. There is a danger far deeper than anything that the King of Kings threatened.'

'Why are you looking like that? It is hateful!'

'Oh yes it is. They are. They are Romans.'

The scarf had fallen from my head and lay loosely round my neck.

'But what can I do? I know nothing of all this.'

'You? You can help to rescue Hellas. Rescue Athens and bring back Delphi.'

It was by the narrowest of margins that I escaped

bursting into laughter. It would not have been a happy laugh. This strange man who was apparently now my guardian was becoming stranger and more unpredictable by the moment. He seemed to be stepping out of the straight, dull road of life in which generally the events of the morrow are easy to foresee from those of today. My mind dipped away towards a memory of a slave we had had, a house slave too, a slave mild even by the standards of our house, where life was more regular even than the ferry. But one day and inexplicably he had started to dance and laugh and would not stop so that at last he had to be restrained, and died so. Something, some thing indeed, had been able to get at him. After his death we had no end of trouble purifying the whole place, for that sort of thing is very disturbing. Now this distinguished and important man was bending towards me and using huge names – Hellas, Aetolia, Achaia – as if they had been pebbles to be tossed about in a game on the beach. He must have read something in my eyes, though I felt then as I have since that the capacity to read things, feelings, opinion, intentions in a face is exaggerated. Also, despite my inclination to laugh, I was afraid. That at least he was able to see, and drew back.

'It is too soon. What would you know about these questions? Have you even heard of the Romans?'

I thought back. My brother? He had talked in my presence about Rome and Carthage. There had been fighting in Sicily.

'A very little, my brother –'

'Demetrios.'

'You knew him?'

'I knew of him. That is not as surprising as you might think. Delphi knows most things, Young Lady. And there you can see some of the topmost buildings climbing up under the Shining Rocks.'

Why describe Delphi? All the world knows how it hangs on the flank of Apollo's mountain. We had reached very nearly to where the road opens up the valley and river below it. People talk about the air of Delphi. They seldom mention the fear that settles on you when you see it, fresh and beautiful and deadly. There are gods hiding everywhere but allowing themselves to be sensed, as if at any moment with a flash of light and a clap of thunder one would start into presence and purpose and power. I had seen Corinth across the water but never been there. So Delphi was my first city, a small and strange one. I tried to extinguish myself.

'Leave your eyes uncovered, Arieka. You must get used to it.'

There were crowds everywhere, and attracted by our soldiers they seemed to clot round our procession. Now the soldiers changed from their solemn walk, with spears lying over the shoulder, and used the butts. They beat the crowd back so that there was shouting and shoving and cursing. Men reached through and touched our brake. It seemed they thought it would bring them

49

luck. A woman held out a string of blue worry beads and, biddable as ever, I touched it with a finger. She screamed in triumph, and I had done the wrong thing. In a second the crowd turned into a howling mob that fought with the soldiers. They struggled to thrust forward beads, a bracelet, an amulet, even a bit of stick so that I might touch it. At the back of the crowd someone was holding a baby over her head where I could see it. Men and women fell. A man was held up by the sheer press. There was blood on his face and his eyes were closed. The driver whipped the horse savagely and our brake surged forward. Little by little we left the crowd and its stench behind. There were open gates before us. We drove through and, glancing back, I saw them close again. Our brake slowed to a walking pace under the shade of tall trees that had even taller cliffs beyond them. Now I could hear the splash and chuckle of water. Ionides gave a huge sigh of relief.

'Come. Let me help you down. Your maid can stay with your boxes.'

It was a building of white stone, columned and porticoed. Ionides led me up the shallow steps to the great two-leaved doors. They moved back silently and we walked through into the coolness of a great hall. A colossal statue of the god stood at the farther end. His face was bleak and beautiful and unbearded as the God Alexander but he was the God Apollo. A thin streamer of incense rose before him from a tripod. He had been dressed for the day in chlamys and cloak. I followed Ionides forward and we each took incense and sprinkled it on the glowing charcoal. The streamer of smoke thickened. Face up and hand lifted, Ionides whispered to the god. Then he led me round behind the effigy and the door opened for us. Ionides' voice became conversational again.

'On the right are the apartments of the Senior Lady. On the left are the apartments, as you might suppose, of the Junior Lady. You will live through here.'

A slave opened yet another door for us, a smaller one.

Light flooded the room. Outside and over the rooftops of the city was the wild side of the mountain but in deep shadow. The slave was opening a window opposite to the first. I turned to watch. As the shutters swung back it was as if the light burst in, too much light, not direct light from Apollo's sun but coming from everywhere, dazzling from what I now saw were buildings in white stone that seemed to lift and tumble up, up rather than down, as if they were escaping the earth and flying like a storm of birds into the sky. And as my eyes became accustomed and distance deepened, I saw how the separate buildings were picked out, adorned as a woman by jewels with delicate patterns of colour which danced round architraves and capitals or glowed in the shade of colonnades. Then, beyond all and as if it held up the deep blue sky, was the precipitous wall of the Shining Rocks.

'Oh it is so beautiful.'

'We Greeks can do that if nothing else. Well, Young

51

Lady, congratulations on your first day of freedom. Welcome to your home.'

I believe I smiled directly at him.

'Thank you, Ionides Peisistratides.'

I looked away, and round the cool shade of the room. There was no pallet or chair, no chest. Ionides laughed.

'Not this room. It is merely your entrance hall. Come.'

The slave hurried across the room and opened yet a further door.

'Go through and examine your quarters, Arieka. I will stay here.'

I am amused when I remember my astonishment and delight — sitting room, bedroom with a bed which made the pallet I was accustomed to seem fit rather for an animal than a girl! There was even a small room dedicated to the toilet which I used with some relief for it had been a long day since dawn. There was a maid's room, smaller and plainer but still more comfortable than the one my parents had thought fit for me. In all the rooms there were objects of which I did not know the use or the name. As if divining what I wanted the slave had been round while I had withdrawn and opened all the shutters so that the cool light of a Delphi late afternoon lay over all. It was a refreshing air, and now I realized that up here among the hills and mountains, even though my new home lay next to the bed of a river so could not at all be described as 'up the mountain', nevertheless the air was distinctly fresher. I saw that in winter it might indeed be cold and that made me aware of the metal bowls in each room which I had not really noticed. They were braziers. Even the servant of the Junior Pythia would be cherished and kept warm. I actually ran back to the entrance hall. Ionides laughed.

'You will soon be accustomed to it. Tell me how delighted you are!'

'I am! I am indeed!'

'Now, if you are at liberty – I think you are, for your official mistress sleeps at this hour – and if the truth be told a good many other hours, too – if, as I say, you are at liberty, there is another room I want to show you. Come.'

We went back into the great hall but turned through a side door which was set in the wall behind Apollo. Steps led down, rather dark steps. Then there was another door and we went through it into the mingled brightness and shade of the colonnade which ran along the side of the building. Then we climbed some steps to a separate building. There were wide doors, open, and then an entrance hall: then more doors. We went through. I supposed it to be a temple.

The room was huge. There was no statue at the other end but open windows. Indeed, at the tops of the walls all round there were openings in which pigeons strutted and cooed. Below them the walls were criss-crossed with wooden boards which left square holes like nesting boxes. But the pigeons had deceived me. They were not nesting boxes.

'Here we are then, Young Lady. Didn't you know? Goats give milk. Kings give gold. What are poets to do? We call it the bookroom. You can use it when you like, since you read. Yes we knew that too. Ever since heaven knows when, and now of course, it's the custom for every author to send a copy to the Foundation. Some of them are – well we have the script of all the plays that have been produced here. I wonder what we should start with?'

Now I had ceased looking at the walls with their rows of what were not nesting boxes I could see that there were rows of sitting places and also large chests lifted on legs. There was not much room between them. Ionides sidled towards the middle one, right in the centre of the great hall.

'Homer, I think.'

He opened the two flaps of the lid. There was a roll on the wooden surface inside, a roll partly opened.

'Could you read the first words to me?'

'I – "The anger sing, O Muse – "'

'Yes. Very good. No. Of course it's not Homer's copy! He very probably couldn't write, at least not with the alphabet. But I tell you what though. This actual copy was sent to us here, generations ago, by my ancestor Peisistratus. You won't have heard of him, you being an Aetolian. But he was chief man of Athens and he decided what version of Homer was the best one, then sent us this copy. Of course you can't say it's his handwriting. A clerk probably did it or perhaps as many as ten or twenty clerks, to make what we call an edition. But you see the little note written at the side? That's what we call a scholiast and I think, indeed I'm very nearly sure, that it was jotted down by Peisistratus' brother – the one who did all those forgeries of our oracles! He was very naughty, but clever. Here, as you can see, he's noted a misspelling. Well so much for the *Iliad*. Now this is your particular favourite, one of the twenty-four books of the *Odyssey*. There's a lot of reading for you in that, isn't there? Then Arctinus – what we call the *Little Iliad*. Personally I don't think it's called that because it's shorter than Homer's work but because it's inferior. You'll read that too I expect. Euripides. The *Ion*. You've heard of Ion? He wasn't my ancestor but he filled the same position as I do here. Euripides wrote the play – this roll here, rather tattered, was the prompt copy and he allowed us to keep it. It's a rather cruel story and I think that perhaps you wouldn't like it. Sophocles. Aeschylus – oh, any tragedian you care to mention. But we don't have the originals of them all, you know. King Ptolemy sent round asking for the originals so that he might copy them for his great bookroom in Alexandria. What we got back were not the originals but the copies. That was really, really wicked. You can see how a decent Greek gets corrupted by eastern influences. Of course, Ptolemy – the first one – was only a Macedonian, which isn't quite – well now what have we here? Ah yes, the Lyrists. Pindar, and I think his master, Simonides, Bacchylides, Erinna – she was a girl like you. Over here though, all on her own, we have – See!'

It was another book box on legs. He laid back the lids and I looked in. There was a book, of course. There was also a plain gold ring and a tuft of rather mousy hair pushed through it. There was an old goose feather, rather crumpled and stained here and there with black.

'The Tenth Muse, Young Lady. Sappho of Lesbos, the island where the head of Orpheus was washed up on the beach after the Wild Women tore him to pieces. I think Sappho is going to be a particular friend of yours. Now don't get the idea you'll meet her in the flesh. She died hundreds of years ago, but what difference does that make? She was a young lady like you, very emotional, very passionate, I think, though she was happiest with girls as I am happiest with – well, I suppose you can guess. Perseus! Could you spare us a moment?'

A young man whom I had not noticed appeared between two of the book chests.

'Ionides. Gracious Lady.'

'This is Perseus, my dear, our infinitely precious slave. Aren't you ever going to accept your freedom, Perseus?'

'And leave this bookroom, Ion? Never! What can I do for you?'

'Could you tell this Young Lady – you know about her – tell her about the book and the rest.'

'Well. The pen is, as the notice says, Sappho's pen. The ring was hers and of course the hair is said to be hers – not very impressive for the Tenth Muse, is it? But then, she was said to be an insignificant little creature – the little brown nightingale of Lesbos, Alcaeus called her. Which of her poems did you wish to see?'

'I don't think we've time for that, Perseus. Just tell us the story.'

'Oh well, she fell in love with a man at last, a fisherman who didn't know his alpha from his beta. Not that that matters of course. But he abandoned her. She was too plain for him. He liked them curvaceous. So she threw herself off a cliff at Leuctra. He sold the book and the ring she'd given him. Poor girl, she'd tried to magic him with it. As for the hair – no I don't think so.'

'Well, there you are, Young Lady.'

'Forgive me, Ion, I'm very busy.'

'Go back to your books about books about books! We'll be content with the makers. Well, Young Lady. I want you to spend as much time as you like here and believe me you'll have plenty of time. There's prose down at that end – Histiaeus, Herodotus, and the fellow who circumnavigated Africa, I forget his name – Alexander's Admiral of the Fleet. Hundreds of books, positively hundreds. But mostly I want you to read the poetry. Particularly the hexameters. I want you to be able to speak in hexameters. But, for now, all you have to do is read, read, read!' He lowered his voice suddenly. 'Arieka! Come, you watering pot, what's the matter? You're free, free, free! Here in this building is man's greatest gift to you, greatest invention! Without it we might still be scratching bulls' heads and pots with ears to them on clay brick! The alphabet, my child, and thank god for the Philistines!'

But I had burst into tears and seemed quite unable to control them. Though whether I was sad or happy or anxious or wholly achieved I find it impossible to say.

III

It was Ionides who took me before the Second Lady. She was not what I had thought a Pythia could possibly be. She was lying on a couch just the way a man does, leaning on one elbow. The first thing anyone would notice about her was that she was enormously fat, fatter even than my nurse had been. She had dewlaps that slumped down as if they might slide right down to the ground at any moment. Her feet were bare and it was the first time in my life that I had seen painted toenails. They matched those on her fingers. I had heard of this, however. My mother had cited it as the sign of 'an unspeakable woman' or a woman whose profession is not to be named. She meant 'female companion', 'hetaera', though I believe there is an even dirtier profession. I do not – or did not – know what it is called.

'Come close, child. Good heavens, you are indeed a child. Fourteen? Fifteen?'

'Fifteen, Gracious Lady.'

'Sit down, child. No, not on the chair. You don't really want to be uncomfortable do you? Try the stool. Isn't that

61

better? I must say, you are not going to stop the traffic in the street, but you have a pretty voice. Do you sing?'

'I don't know, Gracious Lady.'

'Don't be silly. Of course you know!'

She was kind enough but firm. I thought for a while.

'Nursery rhymes. Nothing more. Country songs, a few, like everyone else.'

'A few notes are very helpful. Grunts will do of course. The occasional wail if you think it appropriate.'

'Gracious Lady?'

'She is a real nestling isn't she, Ionides? Where did you find her?'

'We should visit the First Lady I think.'

'Go along then. That'll be all, child.'

'Gracious Lady –'

'Yes?'

'When do you want me to start?'

'Start what?'

'Serving you.'

'You are not serving me, child. You are to serve the god. That's the right form, isn't it, Ion?'

'She hasn't been told much yet. May we go now?'

The Gracious Lady rolled heavily on to her back, stared at the ceiling and seemed to ignore us with point. Ionides bowed and spoke.

'We take our leave then.'

I followed him out and crossed to the opposite door. He laid one finger on his lips and opened it. A doorman stood at ease inside. He came to attention when he saw us. Ionides nodded and led me on. The great living room of the First Lady was still darkling, the shutters bolted. Ahead of us I could just make out a figure, seated on a chair. It seemed to be looking at us. We waited. When the voice came it was like a thread of sound.

'Ionides?'

'I am here. Do I call you Gracious Lady today? Or do I call you Mother?'

'I am the Pythia.'

'I bring you the child. The one I spoke of.'

'Let her come close.'

'Reverend Mother, we cannot see.'

'I said let her come close. So. Give me your hand, child.'

'Here, Reverend Mother.'

'Let me feel your face. You have much boy in you, neither one thing nor the other. That might please him. Do you dream? I said do you dream?'

'Yes.'

'Do you remember your dreams?'

'No, Reverend Mother.'

'It is not for you to call me that. Gracious Lady will do well enough. Later it will change. Do you understand?'

'No, Gracious Lady.'

'Ionides, her mouth is too small. It will be torn.'

'You still believe the power will come again?'

'Do you?'

'No.'

63

'Gracious Lady –'

'What is it, child?'

'My mouth torn – Why am I here?'

'You should have told her, Ionides.'

'I thought it better left to you.'

'Not the other one?'

'I spit me of her.'

'Child, stay where you are. Ionides, open the shutters.'

Presently a long and opening shaft of daylight moved across the room. She was dressed in white and her head was covered in white, all but her face. Her eyes were fixed and only looked where her head turned. It was difficult to believe that they did not see. They had no what we call pin and web, a hardening of the eye's very material. They shone and you would have said pierced but they did not move. As for the rest of her face, it was the very image of age, and stripped down next to the bone.

'Child, you have been chosen for a rare post. Sometimes there is only one Pythia, usually two, but now and then, when the future is blind and dark as my eyes, there are three. In due time you will be the third Pythia.'

I don't know what I said or did. Ionides told me that I was crying out about not going down into *that place* and he had a hard job to hold me from running away anywhere. I came to myself a little and when he felt me stop struggling he let me go. The Pythia spoke behind me and I turned to her.

'Gracious Lady –'

'It is no use, child. Whatever you call him, he has us in his hands. It is simpler to go with the tide. He is merciful to his own. When it became too much he took away my sight so that I should not see him. But that was long ago. Perhaps I dreamed it. Certainly my sight has gone. But now you know why you are here. Be strong and perhaps the god will not demand a torn mouth or blind eyes from you. Be strong. Wise men will take care of you. For the rest, guard your virginity. The god himself will direct them and woe betide you if you transgress. I will not be long, for I am older than any woman should have to be. Prepare yourself.'

'I don't know how – or for what!'

'Ionides knows how or says he does. For me, all that is long ago. Too long ago. I expect, though, he will tell you to read books until scraps of other people's words come up in your speech like a sweet vomit.'

'I rescued you from what you were taught to call home, Arieka. Now you must do as I say. I am your guardian and shall not be unkind to you, believe me. Remember I have already given you a bookroom!'

'Ionides knows everything, child. You will never see round him. Even I, after all these years have never met such a man. I think I know what he wants but I cannot be sure. All I will tell you is that a good workman pays attention to his tools. You will be kept clean and bright and slightly oily. And sharp.'

'I shall keep her simple, charming, innocent –'

'Credulous –'

'Now, who is being clever? You must forget that word, Arieka, as I shall have to forget your name. It is a sacrilege to call the Pythia by her given name. We must all forget it, little one. I shall call you that when we are alone.'

'You will do yourself no good by teasing her, Ionides. When she is inducted she will be the Pythia and don't forget it. She will belong to the god, not to you.'

'I am abashed, Reverend Mother.'

She laughed.

'That is another thing I am unable to believe. Goodbye for today, child. Come and visit me often. I enjoy the scent of simple country flowers.'

'I will bring you some, Reverend Mother.'

'A good girl, Ionides. You see?'

'I do indeed. Come, little one and Pythia that is to be.'

I followed him back to what he had told me was my apartment. Once there he told me that we ought to eat something and might he do so with me? I was overcome by the day's journey, the bookroom and now the thought of not just sitting stiffly upright on a chair but eating with a man – but he was my guardian and I imitated the Second Lady as best I could. The slave who had opened the door for us had disappeared but came back almost at once, and before I was properly reclined, with bread and olives, slices of cucumber and the mildest goat's cheese that I had ever tasted. There was wine too. He offered it to me and I did not know what to do. Ionides spoke.

'I think three to one, Gracious Lady.'

Obedient to my gesture of assent the slave mixed the wine and water, set the cups on either table then withdrew. He had not made a sound. Even when he poured the wine there was no clink of silver against silver, only the faint sound of water pouring into the wine.

'Any questions?'

'No. Yes. Who are you?'

He understood what I meant.

'You know that I am your guardian. I am also the Warden of the college of priests – for we have priests of every god here in Delphi – and I am also myself the High Priest of Apollo. I am concerned that the oracle of Apollo, those instructions, those answers which Apollo gives to questions through the mouth of his Pythia, concerned that the oracle should return to its original state of purity and sanctity. If Apollo will not do it . . .'

There was a long pause while he ate and drank, the sentence hanging uncompleted in the air. At last he touched his lips with a napkin and spoke.

'He will, of course. But when and how and through whom and to what end – for an end is very desirable. Necessary. Can you understand what I mean?'

'I think so. You want true prophecy.'

'I want you to help.'

I spoke simply and from my heart.

'I would do anything, anything in the world to help you.'

'I believe you. Bless you, child. Delphi is the centre of the world. Once, I should say, Delphi was the centre of the world. In those days Athens was the intellectual and artistic centre of the world. I want them, both places, revived. Oh yes, the city of Delphi is well enough. Here we are an enclave, a small protected place where there is a level of civilization, a level of sophistication which is to be found nowhere else in the whole world. But the centre no longer speaks. The Pythia is silent. Men and women dare to ask silly questions that are an insult to the oracle: "What shall I call my unborn son?" "Where shall I find the brooch I lost?" The answers are as trivial as the questions. We need the old voice that men would accept as the voice of god. Of the god Apollo.'

'You said "If Apollo will not do it – "'

'Wait. I have seen a Roman legion you see. I was present, a spectator at the sacrifice. Six hundred men moving as one man, silent, slow, deadly. They make fools of us all. Did you know their javelins have a point of soft iron? They will pierce flesh but bend on a shield. So the javelin is useless for throwing back. Neat, isn't it? The enemy, naive creatures that they are, throw sharp, shiny javelins that can be thrown back. There's many a barbarian that has been killed by his own javelin. Before they've recovered, the Romans are on them, thrusting with their huge shields and thrusting with the broad, short swords at the enemy's groin, the one place any man will protect no matter what, and, before he's recovered, that short, sharp broadsword is up and stuck between his breastplate and his chinstrap, clean through his throat. Then the legion moves on one pace and repeats the process. Simple. They'll conquer the world. So we need Apollo to hearten us and advise you. You see?'

'Yes, I do see. What are we to do?'

'Make the god do what we want.'

'Who can compel the gods?'

'Any man – or woman.'

'You?'

'No, not really. I can contribute to the process that is all. Others must move him – them. You see, I don't believe in them.'

I still don't know how serious he was. Or, if I put it another way, for how long this would be the claim he was putting forward, the tune he was singing this week, his present mode. The claim suited him at the time. He needed to shock a naive girl and he certainly did. That some people did not believe in the gods was common knowledge. But these people were supposed to live somewhere else and be so outrageous as to be inhuman. If you ask how human our family was, down there by the sea, with its brutal father and obedient mother, its children happy always to get away, I would have to reply by asking you how happy you think Greece is or was, Greece, Hellas in totality? Certainly we all feared the gods. You couldn't be sure of any god being on your side unless it was small and personal as a good-luck charm. So when I first heard a grown man declare his disbelief I was not so much frightened as shocked and disbelieving in his disbelief. But the shock gave place to bewilderment at what he said next.

'Well, yes, yes. Of course I do. I am incurably flippant. Don't trouble yourself.'

'No.'

'We do need him. Yes. It's so difficult a question one should be able to put it on one side. Let's do that. Are you willing?'

'Anything.'

'It's a question of hexameters. Um-tiddy um-tum.'

'I don't understand you at all.'

'You believe Homer was inspired by the muse – by Apollo – by the god? Of course you do, like everyone else. Yet they – people, I mean – expect the god to reply to a question, "Look in the back cupboard, dear, on the left-hand side." Of course that's not the voice of god! In the old days, when Hellas was great, the replies to questions came in hexameters, poetry, elevated speech, because the questions were elevated ones. "How shall we defend the gods of Hellas against their enemies?" Or "Since we cannot truckle to the Persians how can we defeat them?" Sometimes the god asked for a man's death. That priest. He was told the battle needed – but you don't know, do you? They gave the reply in hexameters.'

'But I could not do that!'

'The god touched you twice. Yes?'

'No. The stories were – made up. Not by me but they escaped from me. Or rather, I let them go.'

'Why are we talking like this? It doesn't really matter what you think. There's a sense in which it doesn't really matter what I think either. All that matters is that we should both move towards the desired end. The first step is the hexameters. If the god should never speak through you, so be it. But the instrument shall be ready. Yes?'

'But the gods are real, aren't they?'

'Yes, yes. Of course. How not? Why make such a meal of the question? You have said it. There are twelve Olympians, with the odd later attachment. But they're like hexameters – like poetry – life is like that. You can make a debate about everything, question everything and anguish over it like, well, Socrates. In that sense he was wise. But do you notice here and there when he stopped people in the street – not his friends but passers-by – they were anxious to get away? It wasn't their world you see. They themselves didn't question each footstep because walking came naturally.'

'I haven't heard about Socrates.'

'And you lived all your life by the road up to Delphi! It's criminal.'

At this Ionides glanced at me and gave a visible start.

'My dear child! What have I been thinking of? You must be dead on your feet! I'll see you again tomorrow after you are rested. Farewell.'

So that was the beginning of freedom. It was strange

71

that I who had had nothing to do, who had thought myself a prisoner, now found I had everything to do and thought myself free! But the strangest feeling of all, and one that grew only slowly, was that I was happy. It was like those times in very early childhood when one is too young to be anything but happy, not seeing threats before they became facts. Ionides did teach me about hexameters and about many other measures too. But I was never alone with any man except him. A man came who taught me how to speak so that a whole roomful of people could hear. He taught me how to make the great movements of the body which are a language and can be read further away than a man's voice can be heard. Another man showed me the flowing script which I use in writing down this. Wrapped, muffled, unrecognizable, I followed Ionides through the streets of Delphi as an obedient and well-mannered wife follows her husband or a girl her father. We saw the temples and treasuries, the empty treasuries, we saw the stadium and the theatre, the streets and alleys, the great houses and the small ones, the beer houses, houses of pleasure and the hostels for travelling men. Every day I spent hours in the bookroom. Sometimes strange men came and consulted with Perseus or eyed poor Chloe where she was yawning, her face carelessly bared. No one bothered to look at me, a muffled figure poring over an unrolled scroll. It was for me an enchantment. After a while, whenever I met Ionides – and he came to the palace of the Pythias almost every day – he would address me with an hexameter and wait, his head on one side, ready to assess the answer. I was very shy at first and could hardly stammer out a phrase as he wanted. But he would say, 'Oh, come along, a half-line, even just an umtiddy um-tum!' Then one day I tried to explain that it wasn't that I didn't want to or didn't know what he wanted, I was shy, that was all – and found myself falling into the measure as easily as slipping into something loose, and he gave a great shout which echoed in the bookroom and brought Perseus running from his cell. Ionides gave me the victor's salute.

'A great step forward!'

After that we sometimes carried on quite long conversations in the measure and I began to think in it as well as speak it. I don't know whether I have recorded anywhere that the Pythia used to give the answer in hexameters. Ionides thought that if only the questions could be made great enough the speech would follow. I was eager to please him as I suppose any girl would be. I planned to get rid of Chloe. She was too pretty. When I told Ionides he agreed. So we sold her to her great relief. I myself was so relieved that I gave her the smaller of the two Egyptian necklaces which had come down from my mother's mother. There was no possibility of my wearing them myself. But I shocked Ionides by this.

'Why, in the name of god?'

'Whenever I used to look at her neck I would think first of the necklace lying round it and second of strangling her.'

'Have you any conception of what that necklace is worth? She could buy her freedom with it! But that old fool who has bought her could make his fortune if he had the wit.'

'She is gone and I want to forget her.'

Ionides showed me another place too. I do not know what to call it. I think the columbarium would be as near as anything. It was a small building and this is because there was a cave behind it, so that you never knew when you were in the open but in a building, or when you were under the earth and in a cave. The cave had been so altered. He instructed me in vivid terms that I was not to speak of anything I saw, ever. Indeed, I don't think he showed me the columbarium because the knowledge of it would be useful to me but because he wanted to impress me with his cleverness and importance. Oh yes, I had seen round Ionides already and liked him all the more for it. Any woman feels all the more secure with a man – with her man, and if Ionides was anyone's man it was mine – when she sees a little further round him and into him than he thinks. Quite a number of men, slaves of course, worked in the columbarium. It was a building with many ladders, or stairs as I learn I must call them. We climbed them all and they were so built that a woman, or for that matter a man, could use them without indecent exposure to below. At the top there were many cages for pigeons and the first time we reached them, a bird fluttered in, rang its bell as it did so, then flopped in the bottom of the cage. Ionides reached in and took a tiny roll of paper from its leg.

'Smyrna. All the way across the Aegean Sea and Attica. Here you are, Ariston, take it.'

'That bird carried a message all the way from Asia?'

'Yes. You see there are places, you've probably heard of them. They like to keep in touch with Delphi, still the centre of the world. And one day –'

'What messages?'

'That's a secret, Young Lady. But you've heard of other oracles besides us? Dodona for instance?'

'Of course.'

'Tegyra, Delos, Patarae? Branchidae, Claros, and Gryneum? Siwa over in Africa?'

'A bird can't fly all the way here from Africa!'

'Of course not. There's measure in all things as your – our – god said – says. You'd need a Phoenix for that.'

'What messages? From the god? Why?'

'The price of corn perhaps. What the tribes are doing. Who's in, who's out, who up, who down.'

'Surely the god doesn't need to be told what is happening!'

'Reminded, shall we say. It's a good theological point. What does the god need to know? After all he needs to know what the question is. Therefore he needs to know something. Therefore there is no reason why he should not need to know what is happening in Asia, or Africa, or Achaia . . .' He paused for a while, '. . . or Rome.'

'I see.'

I thought I did see.

'I don't think you do, child. Still you are safe from too much knowledge until you are fifty.'

'But I should be an old woman!'

'The Pythia used to be an old woman. No not like our First Lady. She's about a hundred. Ten decades. Judging by the state of the Second Lady, I think the process will have to be hurried up.'

'How much?'

'Would you accept forty?'

'Thirty.'

'Thirty then. You and I, privately, will agree that the Third Lady in waiting shall become the Second Lady when she reaches the advanced age of thirty. First, Second, Third Lady – you know, my dear, I always feel when I talk about the three Ladies as if I am talking about a particularly uxorious, or should I say gynoecious, potentate. Now, this afternoon you observe I am not in a very pious mood. Indeed the god was brusque with the First Lady, not to say brutal. He raped her. I am shocking you. Don't mind, my dear, we've made an honest trio of you. That, by the way, and to change the subject, is the fountain of Castalia. You are supposed to drink from it before you prophesy. I'm afraid it's sometimes not very clean. You see the little building built across it? You go in there and a small boy gives you to drink out of what ought to be the gold cup donated by Queen Olympias in thanksgiving for the birth of her son. Unfortunately your compatriots of that time re-

76

moved it along with some other trifles such as a life-sized image of the Pythia in solid gold. The history of Delphi is to be read in the chopping and changing over the nature of the cup you will drink from. You'll find the cup we have at the moment is made of wood and secured by an iron chain. It has the words "A present from Dodona" incised on it. No, I'm wrong. My memory! This is Cassotis of course. The spring of Castalia is where you bathe. It's fearsomely cold – comes right out of the frozen heart of the mountain and is given up to the god very grudgingly. Now, if you look, you'll only see a trickle. That's why there aren't any prophecies in the three months of winter. You won't be able to see the ritual, in fact, for another two months or so. Of course, if someone of heroic stature, a pharaoh, say, or a Mithridates, wanted a quick reply, it's astonishing how adaptable the mountain can be. This year, by the way, is a festival year – one in four or eight according to the oracle given at the spring solstice. It's very good for tourism.'

'Tourism?'

'Groups of travellers who come to see our – your – sights. I'm afraid they keep the economy alive, but you can't expect them to do so in the winter months. I dare say, though, we may see the first gorgeous butterfly of spring in a month, there are always a few early ones.'

It took me a long time to understand that by 'spring butterflies' he meant tourists, these quaint travellers who want to 'see the world', as it is expressed. The general route was through the Peloponnesus to Athens, then back

to Corinth and across our ferry. It was thus, and with still
most of the month to go before the solstice, that I saw my
first Roman. There was a small crowd of Delphians who
seemed to be following very slowly an even smaller group
of men. Ionides held me back until they had passed and
muttered the word 'Roman' in my shrouded ear. The Roman looked very mild and not at all threatening. He was
wearing a most complex robe of white linen with a purple
stripe running through it for a border. He wore no jewellery round his neck and was as clean-shaven as a young
man, though clearly he was quite an old one. He had a
close-cropped thatch of iron-grey hair. His only ornament
was a gold seal ring. A Delphian priest of Zeus was speaking very slowly to him in a strange language.

'Latin,' said Ionides. 'A language with too much grammar and no literature.'

'Can he not speak Greek?'

'Only those who are well-educated. Metellus is not all
that well-educated. As you saw, he has a smile. That is
permanent as long as he is in Greece. They, the Romans,
admire our arts and crafts but hold us, ourselves, in contempt. It is a paradox and never ceases to annoy me. As
you saw, he was smiling at people. That is merely to conceal his contempt. They are strong, that is all. That they
will conquer the world is a nightmare that haunts me.
One must have a little corruption. Since human law cannot be perfect one must be able to bend and turn. They do
not understand this. There is a passion for what they call

78

"honesty" in some parts of the world but it is always limited to the people who claim it. The Hebrews, for instance, and the Romans. Their public servants, or at least a great many of them, neither give nor take bribes. Often even a rich man is condemned by the courts. Quite often a poor man goes free. They do not see that where all men take bribes and give them, nobody does!'

'I do not understand that.'

'You will.'

Indeed I did. I had not long to wait. But more of that later. The small crowd which had been following Metellus and his guide had moved on. The most remarkable thing about them, I thought, was how respectful to Metellus the front of the crowd had been and yet how the back of it sniggered. The back of a crowd, according to Ionides, is where the true nature of an international relationship may be studied in little. All I can say in that case is that judging by the crowd following Metellus, Greeks envy Romans their power and distinction but will use them for Greek ends wherever they can. The Romans do not trust us and they are wise not to do so.

It was on that walk that we came to the temple of the Cave. The Cave is where Apollo fought the python, the dragon, and conquered her, him, it. This was where, when he had slain the creature, he took over the oracle for himself and appointed a woman – a Pythia, a female dragon! – to utter the oracle. I must say that in god-haunted Delphi with its bright air, its splendour both natural and civic, the temple of the oracle is a daunting place. It is set aside as much as a building can be in such a crowded place. It is low, too, and seems to crouch. We stopped when we came within sight of the portico, or at least I stopped, and Ionides did when he realized I was no longer with him.

'What is the matter?'

'That is it.'

'Yes.'

There was an air, no doubt of that. I cannot describe it. Perhaps it was simple, unqualified fear, as if the portico had figured always in my nightmares though I knew I had never seen the place before.

'Want to go home.'

'And disappoint me?'

So he knew! He was as willing as any Roman to use his power.

'No, of course I don't.'

'You disarm me. I wish – but there it is.'

'I know. You don't have to explain.'

We were silent for a while, watching the facade.

'Well, Lady?'

'Can't you see I'm shuddering? I can't seem to stop. Teeth chattering.'

'I was right then.'

'I –'

Suddenly I felt my body turn of its own. I started to run, but before I had gone more than a yard or two he had me by the wrist.

'It means going back to your parents.'

There was a time, I do not know how long, during which I fought with my shudders. Gradually his hold on my wrist relaxed.

'Brave girl.'

That made me laugh. He let go of me entirely.

'That's better. If you laugh like that then you've won.'

'Is there any other way to laugh?'

'Oh yes.'

'It came up out of the earth.'

'Where else? Come!'

'No nearer!'

'Make yourself. I won't touch you.'

There was a time in which I examined the fear. It was round and solid and heavy, was an impossibility lying between me and that place.

'Remember. I rely on you.'

I suppose all men have this small craft when they know they have found the weakness of a woman. It is unfair and perhaps, though I do not know, it is unmanly. But then, how can it be unmanly? Perhaps it is a man's weakness. Men and women – we are of little account.

'I am ready.'

Together we walked forward. The shuddering had gone. The fear was still there, but mixed, I do not know how or why, with grief. It was grief about women I think. Grief for them as instruments to be played on by gods or men. Beyond the portico some steps led down, but not very far.

It looked like a little hall. There was some light, not just from the steps, but I now saw two small lamps were burning either side of the steps and about halfway down.

'Go down and stand.'

Obediently and accepting my fear I went down and stood at the bottom of the steps. Here there were no lights. It was a hall, a plain one. And dark – not entirely dark, for daylight filtered down the steps even in winter and in the shade of the mountains but a darkness only just qualified, modified by dim light. Where was the brightness of Apollo – where was the Sun God?

Now my eyes were a little accustomed to the dimness. The hall was not entirely bare. There was an opening in the wall before me. It was black. That, then, was the entrance to the adytum, the place of the tripod and the brazier, the gap going down into the earth whence the air of oracular utterance was breathed forth to become the breath of the Pythia on her tripod as she writhed and cried out when the god had her in his hands. That was the fate of little Arieka whom nobody loved.

I turned back at last and joined Ionides in the street.

'Well?'

'I shall die of terror.'

'They don't, you know.'

'They have their mouths torn, though.'

'That is figurative. You will be the most honoured woman in Greece – in the world.'

'Perhaps the Romans will consult this oracle.'

'They have done so. The story is that the oracle used to be consulted in political matters – what alliances should be made, what wars undertaken or stopped. They say that kind of oracle, that kind of question, ceased hundreds of years ago. It isn't true. It's just that those questions are asked in secret. Why give your enemy information which might be useful to him? Mankind learns, you see.'

'Have you read Herodotus?'

'Yes, child, I have read Herodotus. Why?'

'I was thinking of the treasure. All that gold! Even just the gold given by Croesus. Where did they keep it?'

'Until your honourable Aetolian or should I say Phocian ancestors removed it, in that entrance hall. Also some down in the adytum, more on either side in accommodation you did not see. The mountain has been excavated on either side of the portico. There are rooms. Nowadays the guardians of the complex live there, but once it was filled on both sides with gifts. Some of them have been donated by Romans. I must say, I think they are – frugal. Perhaps our dear masters did not get the answers they wanted, though I can hardly believe that.'

But my thought had returned to my own affairs.

'I dread the day.'

'Think of yourself as a soldier. A Greek soldier – Thermopylae, Marathon, even Salamis! Your dread is that of a soldier who knows that one day he will have to face his fear – but not just yet.'

*

83

It was thus that life went on. The First Lady died, though according to Ionides it was difficult to tell. She had not lain on a bed for years but always sat upright on her chair, her bright unseeing eyes open, her skeleton's hands folded in her lap. At the last she neither ate nor drank and one day an attendant brushed against her and she fell over sideways and – I am assured – more or less fell apart. But by the time the Second Lady who was now the First Lady had seen her body, as by custom she was bound to do, and after I, the Third Lady who was now the Second Lady had attended her to that gruesome ceremony, life went straight back to being what it was, except that I had even more splendid quarters, more servants and gifts for which I had done nothing.

Ionides said I should accept them.

'They commit you to nothing,' he said. 'People are investing not in you but in the truth. The story of the half-cooked fish and the child who recovered at your touch have been inflated. You will be a rich woman in your own right, my dear. The oracle benefits. News of your suitability for mediating between the physical universe and the spiritual cosmos has brought it a shower of gifts from people who do not want to ask a question at the moment but feel they may do – kings, sitting as they always do on shaky thrones, rich businessmen, uneasy key men from caucuses, tyrants and terrorists. It is the future, and like the rest of us Greeks they are condemned to move backwards towards it, until the last bit when the Ferryman takes them backwards beyond all question.'

'I wish –'

'What? Come! It is unusual for our Second Lady to have a wish of her own.'

'Never mind.'

'I am still your guardian and I insist. Come, child, do you want to be disobedient for the first time?'

'I was wishing I had a home. What I think of as a home. That place down there by the sea wasn't a home for anyone. I must have been a changeling. There's nothing of my father, my honoured father in me. A home. A place that welcomes you and people there who wait for your coming with – love. That's what I want. A home.'

'Does not the part you are to play in the story of the nations, of mankind – doesn't that do instead?'

'Of course not. To begin with, I don't believe in it – don't believe anything I can say will influence anybody.'

'It will be your voice but the god's words.'

'Shall I tell you? I have prayed. Once, when I was in great shame and grief and sorrow, I prayed. I really did. You'll remember the occasion so I won't elaborate. But the gods deserted me. Or rather I saw them going away. They were there all right. But I among all people – they had turned their backs on me.'

'Have you ever heard of Moses?'

'Who?'

'A great Hebrew leader. He gave them law and worship and so on. Ritual too. He begged to see the god but his god wasn't having any of it. He knew, you see, that Moses would simply die at the sight. A bit like Semele and Zeus. So he hid Moses in a crack in the rock, covered him with his hand and passed by and all Moses saw of his god was the back-parts. But he hadn't deserted Moses. By no means.'

'They turned their backs to me.'

'So you saw their back-parts. Perhaps they'll cover you with their hands and put you in the crack at the oracle and –'

'Don't say that!'

'Arieka, I assure you, you are highly favoured among women. Why not, pray? You are *the* – or *a* – Pythia and I am the High Priest of Apollo. We can say what we like and if anyone complains we can say we are inspired.'

I made the apotropaic sign. 'God send the gods don't hear you!'

'At midday the gods are asleep if they have any sense. I can feel the spring, though. Another month and it'll be time for the Questions. Though what sort of a noise that fat slug of a bitch will make, Apollo alone knows. She's killing herself with honeycakes. We'll have to carry her to the oracle and throw her down the steps.'

'Ionides Peisistratides!'

IV

But the gods had other plans. The new First Lady died that very night in her snorting sleep. It is not good luck for the people to know too much about the living and dying of the Pythias. They are there, or not. People there, having accustomed themselves, though unconsciously, to refer to the Two Ladies now found themselves having consciously to refer to The Lady, concerning whom those with any knowledge of the oracle's history would find themselves exclaiming amusedly 'It's quite like old times!' The old times for the oracle were some six thousand years ago at a modest computation. There was, as well as this, a matter of no more than two weeks between the death and the festival of the spring solstice, combined with the Games and the Questions, a hundred other questions and the transfer of my few personal belongings from the apartments of the Second Lady to those of the First.

I was terrified. The terror was not of this world. As far as this world was concerned nothing made much difference. I was a shrouded figure, the one woman now in Delphi whose face was never bared. I was aware of a rumour that I was younger than any First Lady had ever been though how young they did not know. But the explanation given was that I was a virgin, not a married woman living apart from her husband, and well on in years – fifty or so. The rumour attached was that I had already given signs of the god's choice. That fresh, bright air of Delphi seemed to be able to create stories out of nothing. For the people did not believe in the Olympians alone. It seemed sometimes that every street corner had its arguing group who swore to the reality of this demon or that, this or that nostrum for either seeing the demon or alternatively not seeing him. My information was that the new First Lady was rumoured to have, literally, eyes in the back of her head. She was said to be accompanied by a whole troupe of demons whose bidding she was compelled to do. Delphi, in fact, was a muck heap of nonsense. I refused to have anything to do with it. To be a Pythia, to be educated in the hexameter in case the god should choose to revert to using it, was trouble enough. I buried myself in the bookroom and spoke to no one but Perseus. Perseus spoke all languages that there are. This did not prevent his Greek from having a curious malformation in which the 'p's became 'k's. It was also thick, so that his 'k' was never sure that it was not a 'kh'. By now when I sometimes spoke – especially if we were discussing books as we frequently were – I would observe a smile flit over his darkling face. Learned and distinguished man as he was, he was still a slave and I did not feel it proper to admit him to such intimacy as I enjoyed – the right word – with Ionides. If we were not married – I mean Ionides and I – if he still had and would always have that shuddering distaste for a woman's flesh which made any physical intimacy out of the question, I doubt if any married couple ever approaches the intimacy of thought and feeling that we sometimes enjoyed – or, and I must make the qualification – that I for my part felt we enjoyed. One day he came to the bookroom when Perseus was hidden away in his own place, trying as usual to make sense of the picture writing on a Cretan brick. Ionides was jubilant.

'First Lady – two things! First – they are bringing the *Ion* of Euripides! You will see your first tragedy! Second, they feel that the death in succession of two Ladies means that the god has a special purpose and need – imagine a god having a need, oh Athens! – a special need of the current First Lady. They are organizing the greatest, most brilliant pomp that Athens has ever sent!'

'A pomp?'

'The city fathers, all the priests of all the gods new and old, the academy, the knights on horseback, have you ever – no of course you haven't! Never mind, and forgive my chatter. Remember I'm an Athenian. The Archon himself will ask the question on behalf of the city. Of course Athens isn't what it was any more than Delphi is. But, never mind, we shall do our best. Once I have found out what question he is asking –' He stopped for a moment.

91

'Don't look so pained my dear, it's quite usual nowadays –'

'That wouldn't please the god. No wonder half Delphi is in ruins and the other half made into hostels for tourists rather than suppliants.'

'I was forgetting myself. Forgive me, First Lady, of course we must have no prior knowledge of the questions. It would be unthinkable.'

'There would be an ox on my tongue.'

'You are very fond of that expression, are you not? It means you are going back to the old fear that you are unworthy. Well. You are a virgin. That disarms any god I believe. It is also supposed to tame wild beasts, prevent drunkenness and ensure good harvests. What have you got to worry about? I wish I was in your case.'

I did not know quite what he meant by that for he was unmarried, and I did not care to ask for an explanation.

'Ionides.'

'What is it?'

'I have been reading.'

'As always. Good. It can do nothing but good. If everyone could read and would read – what an outburst of wisdom!'

'I've been reading about the oracle. This time it was about the legend and saying that the Old Religion was woman's. Saying that some of the images were buried and have been dug up – monstrous fat women –'

'So they have. You know there are oracles everywhere. Not as famous as us of course, but still useful to their own locality. This morning when the assembly agreed in Athens –'

'This morning?'

'Have you forgotten our pigeons? Why! We knew what had been decided in Athens sooner than the Athenians knew in their own suburbs.'

'But who –?'

'Come, my dear! Athens has an oracle too. One foot cannot walk by itself.'

A great and frightening light flooded my mind.

'So *that* –'

'Is how it is done. Yes, Arieka, that is how it is done. I had not meant to tell you but of course I am fundamentally a blabbermouth. It was too much to keep to myself. All the oracles everywhere – some one pigeon flight, some a dozen pigeon flights away; but all bound for Delphi!'

'It is outrageous. All those people!'

[A passage of manuscript is missing at this point.]

V

I had taken to wandering in Delphi, a shrouded and unrecognizable woman going about the market and trying the vegetables and cheeses on sale. No one paid any attention to me. It was thus I was even able to approach the building of the oracle itself, noting that the portico remained unpainted. I climbed the steps and looked down those that led into the appalling interior. It was down there, in the adytum, that the compelling vapour was said to issue from the deep cleft in the rock – that same cleft, it may be, which had been the lair of Pytho, whom Apollo slew in hand-to-hand combat. I myself was now in some sense Pytho himself, but humbled, forced into the obedient servant of the oracle, the human instrument whose mouth he might tear as he would. Daylight penetrated some distance down those stairs, but dimly. There were recesses on either hand and stone seats in them. I hoped devoutly that those seats would be filled with living persons when I went down. Ionides would be there, I knew – nearest to the sacred tripod, where I must sit, and the glowing charcoal on which I must heap the dried laurel leaves then inhale their smoke. I turned away. The day would come soon enough. Why run to meet it?

But Delphi was making an effort, there was no doubt about that. The Foundation might have no means of support other than the credit of the heavens, but each individual trader seemed determined to show the tourists 'the real Delphi'. There was paint everywhere, spring flowers not just for sale but put up as decorations. The great day rushed upon us, the seventh day of the month. At dawn Ionides arrived, craving an audience but marching in before I had granted it. He accepted a mouthful of wine.

'The pomp has been received at your father's house, did you know? It's most generous. I suppose that at last he's decided he's proud of you. The position, my dear, the position! So he has put up as many people as possible. The Megarans will be coming along the shore then up the road. Corinth will be here, of course. Now. I think we have time to go over the questions.'

'But I'm not supposed to know them!'

'Do you want to make things difficult? The most important are the city ones of course. Athens first. Will we – will they – preserve the age-old freedom of the city? We have to say yes, of course. The usual escape clause, as you know. There's a Roman, officially a private citizen. I only found out this morning that he's coming. "Just a tourist." A likely story!'

'If he claims to be a private citizen, let us treat him that way.'

'Alas no. The realities of power, my dear. Our power is spiritual. Rome's power is quite another matter. So though he pretends to be private we'd better be ready with something about the sucklings of the she-wolf. You've no idea how credulous the Romans are. That question could be worth millions of those gold coins of which we have so few.'

'The Foundation has ten.'

'He wants to know whether he will achieve his ambition. You note the singular noun, ambition! He wants to be consul, they all do. They're really like the Spartan kings, come two at a time to keep an eye on each other. Not a bad idea at that, it mostly works.'

'You don't need me, Ionides. Why not give the oracles yourself?'

'Ha ha, very funny, First Lady. He's Metellus Cimber and he wants to know about an aristocratic young friend of his, Caesar. Which of the two of them will rise higher. My goodness, I have heard of Caesar, to say nothing of this man Cimber.'

'I haven't.'

'Naturally. I have a feeling in my bones – oh no! I shouldn't say that! Why keep a Pythia and do the shouting oneself? You had better be entirely ambiguous about these two Roman lads. Does anything suggest itself to you?'

'Apollo has never been so far away. I don't even see his back-parts.'

'In Latin, Cimber ought to mean a man from up north,

more nearly under the Pole Star. As for Caesar – something to do with a cut, I think. What a foul language Latin is! Could you say Caesar will be a cut above the Pole Star? What is the matter?'

'I don't like it. Ionides, you've never understood. I believe – even though they turned their backs on me, I believe. In Delphi I feel the gods present if it's only for other people. This is all – I would call it blasphemy and I don't mean the blasphemy which might be punished by the law, though that's bad enough. But this – it will be punished by the gods themselves!'

'That is exactly as it should be, my dear. Do you not understand that I wish devoutly that it might be true – that when you go down there the god will really speak through you – I wish it but I don't believe it.'

'If you wish, why bother to prepare all these questions?'

'Look. I speak in all seriousness. I am a flimsy creature, not solid like you. But when you go down those steps and climb on to the sacred tripod, you are free. You are the freest woman in Hellas – in the world! You will say what you will say. You will only resort to our answers rather than the god's if you find nothing but silence. I shall be sitting in the nearest niche to you where there is still a glimpse of the day. I shall have my tablets and stylus. If you speak not out of our agreement but out of the god's promptings, I will write your words down and proclaim them to the crowd even though they should say "Ionides is a false priest and should be destroyed here and now!"'

So he said, convincing himself. Ionides was even better at convincing himself than convincing other people, and he was good at that. As he spoke there was a warmth and passion in his voice that was most affecting and after it his glottis went up and down no less than three times.

'I see.'

'Forgive me speaking so strongly. But I had a sudden feeling that you thought the oracle was *rigged*. No, no, my dear. I speak with the tongues of men. You should speak with the tongues of the Holy Messengers. But –' and here he smiled his wonderful, sad smile – 'If we cannot have the one let us at least have the other.'

'Very well. I'll say no more –'

'Oh but your contribution on this level is essential – quintessential! You must live on two levels! I, alas, have only one! We'll leave the Roman question since it seemed to disturb you. Forget it and live – quintessentially on two levels. There! Understand, my dear, that people still ask political questions. The Roman question is political. But if indeed you find silence when their question is put to you, do you suppose that we can risk having the Pythia say anything she likes over a question that affects the whole world? Silence would be best ideally, if the god does not speak. But, then, who would consult the oracle?'

'I see.'

'Sometimes I myself wish I was some rustic fellow tending the village oracle – some old biddy who reads palms and divines in running water, or even some fellow who goes about the dry countryside dowsing for it! Anything sometimes to break out of the sad rational world! Now, about Athens. Of course the freedom question is for show and has to be answered about how free Athens is, now the children are taking care of their mother. Everybody will know what that means. But the real question is which side to back so as to keep the Hellespont open to Athenian shipping for corn. Make the wrong choice and they'll starve. Well, never mind. I can see the situation is being almost too much for you. I'll answer that one, though the god knows it's a toss up between two dictators. May I advise? I have complete faith in your integrity. But it is a public and dramatic occasion. I myself am prone sometimes to drama which becomes melodrama. Do be simple, my dear, a homely, rather slow creature, everybody's aunt, if not mother. If anything goes wrong I can have the shawms sounded and that would give us both a breathing space. In any case, remember the most important thing is that you can be as slow as you like, take half an hour to get yourself settled on the tripod, remember you have all the time in the world. In fact' – and he smiled again – 'even though you will be invisible, it's *your* show!'

He rose to go but stopped and turned to me again.

'I nearly forgot! Can you stand the smell of burning laurel?'

'I don't know. Do I have to stand it? Don't I have to be overcome by it?'

'Perhaps we ought to try it – how foolish of me! Of

course the First Lady had been using it before I was born and the Second never got near that tripod. What are we to do?'

'Once again, I don't know. I don't seem to know much, do I?'

'There isn't time. We shall have to chance it. How I wish it were a simple matter of incubation.'

'Which is –?'

'A Latin term. The suppliant goes to sleep in the precinct and dreams, that is all. Very simple. Well, my dear, dare I say "Good luck"?'

He bowed.

They sounded the shawms outside the palace of the Pythias. I went, shrouded, to the vehicle which by tradition I never saw. I was helped into it and supported. It moved on brazen wheels and I knew, though I did not see them, that it was hauled over the noisy cobbles by young men who were honoured by the task. There was a noise almost as loud as the shawms from the wheels and when it stopped a third noise was a kind of sea roar from the people. Their voices beat in on my ears so that I was hard put to it not to cover them with my hands as well as the material of my scarf. But the Pythia must remain in public a shrouded figure, even her hands folded under the maiden garments with which she approaches her celestial bridegroom. I never saw the famous Athenian procession which anyway had stopped at the entry to Delphi since there was no room for them inside. But I heard the roar dwindle into near silence, which was filled with the breathing of people and the stamp and wicker of horses far off. Then into that breathing silence the shawms sounded four times. As the sound of the last note died away I felt a hand search for mine and take it and the voice of the High Priest of Apollo murmur in my ear, 'Come'.

I was lifted down from whatever vehicle it was, and I heard the sound of the chosen goat being sacrificed.

'Hold my hand. The steps begin just in front of you.'

I felt for the step like the blinded creature I was, leaning into his arm for support and reassurance. One step. Two.

'Slowly.'

Another step. More. It seemed to me that the breathing of living creatures was bearing in on me. I found my own breath coming quick. My heart was thudding.

'Stay.'

I stood and his hand left me. Even inside my headscarf I kept my ears shut in desire of ignorance and safety. Down here was the dark. Behind there the noise of the crowd was as it might be waves turning over on the beach of the very gulf itself. But the gulf was far away. Here was nothing but other. I felt round with my hands, stretched out my arms, knew I must not move or I should be lost. In sudden terror I clutched at the scarf and wrestled with it till it came away from my face. But there was still nothing to see. Suddenly my whole body began to shudder, not the skin with its surface movements but the deep flesh and bone, a repeated convulsion that turned me sideways, then round. My knees struck the solid earth and I felt cloth and flesh tear.

'Evooee!'

It was the god. He had come. What was this? A yell, my chest pumping out air, the muscles convulsed again.

'Evooee-ee, Bacche!'

What was this? The drumming died in my ears and I heard from that sun-drenched crowd before the portico a stricken and sudden silence. The god. What god, which god, where? Suddenly the whole tomb place was full of rolling, rollicking laughter that went on and on, louder and louder and I knew as my body worked like some automaton that it came through my own mouth. Then, as sudden and horribly as it had come – no, not horribly that brazen clangour – but as suddenly as it had come there was silence. The shawms broke it and when they ceased the crowd itself took up the cry of the two gods and then the silence came again. I found I was kneeling, my two hands taking some of my weight before me. For a measureless time I was too exhausted for fear. But I spoke to the god who had laughed: 'Have mercy!'; and it was so strange to feel that same mouth which had opened and bled at the passage of the god's voice could now make words for a poor woman on her knees. Whoever god have mercy. My maiden's clothes were heavy on me, clinging, and I guessed that they were soaked with sweat. I opened my eyes and saw. There was light now. It was not what would be called light in the world of the sun but down here in the under-world it might be seen by, or seen itself if there was nothing else about. It was a glow from the brazier; and with a flinch that moved me on the floor I saw the skeletal otherworldly creature standing on its three legs, the sacred tripod. I felt it was the god who helped me then to crawl towards it and lay hands on the thick, cool bronze of its ankles. I climbed a mountain, groaning, sometimes wailing but now there was no escape. The god would have me there in the holy seat whether I would or no, oh yes, it was a rape, this was Apollo who fitted me into the seat, twisted me anyway he would, then left me. I felt brave all of a sudden when he left me and I shouted out with my own voice though it hurt my jaws and even my lips.

'One mouth or the other!'

The rollicking laughter came again.

Then as suddenly as it had all happened, it stopped. I mean the madness in my mind stopped as my heart and lungs eased. I was sitting in a seat, however uncomfort-able, held up and away from the unseen floor. The faintly glowing charcoal in the round brazier a foot below my face looked like a full moon rising through mist. I had never felt so clear-headed. This was a woman's place, the Pythia's place. They trespassed, that over-male god, those two male gods coming in and forcing their cries of wor-ship through my twisted mouth which still tasted blood. The simple answer to madness was just this: to refuse to do their bidding. I sat, now warming my hands in the gentle heat from the brazier. What had they made of it, that crowd out there? The shrouded Pythia descends into the adytum. There is a pause, then the two shouts more male than female and after that the laughter. Then 'One mouth or the other!' They will argue about that.

I could see more clearly now. There was daylight at the steps and the niches empty, all but one where I could just see the knees of Ionides projecting. He was crouched back in his niche. Had the laughter frightened him? Did he still believe nothing? Now the shape of his head appeared. He was staring into my darkness. He spoke in a conversational voice and there was no emotion in it at all.

'A question from our Roman guests who agree that their names should be spoken aloud. They are Julius Caesar and Metellus Cimber. They ask the god which of them shall rise higher.'

It was in my mind to laugh. As if a god could care about their affairs and competitions! But I knew that if I laughed it would be my own laughter and not the Pythia's. In my silence I could hear the crowd laughing. They took it as a jest the Roman guests had made to amuse them; good, kind guests that they were! Then I heard the High Priest of Apollo transmit to the crowd the answer which he had not heard and the Pythia had not given.

'There will be a competition and one will be a cut above the other.'

There was laughter and applause. It was as if Ionides and the two Roman guests were playing a game at a party.

But I myself was the Pythia, had given no reply – and I had forgotten the laurel leaves! They were there, in flange-like depressions round the central charcoal of the brazier! I put my hand into the nearest pile. It was dust, the leaves broken up and ground down. I was about to scatter the leaves when I saw that a tenon or bar had been left unlatched across the front of the tripod. Quite clearly it was meant to be brought across my waist and latched into the other side of the tripod. Without it, if the leaves made me dizzy I might easily fall forward with my face in the charcoal. I was frightened again all of a sudden. Everything was unknown, nobody had warned me. It was part of the ritual of any oracular sanctuary to take risks with the devoted – what else could that word mean? The goat had taken a risk. He had lost. Were the gods supposed to protect me? Did he think Apollo would have touched me on the shoulder and murmured in my ear 'Do please remember to latch the safety bar, dear. We don't want you to burn your face.' Or he might want me to, my father all those years ago saying, 'Well your face will never be your fortune, dear.' Apollo might think there was a joke there for the Immortals to enjoy. She had said it, that nameless Pythia sitting in this same chair, her chair, my, our chair, 'You'll be killed by the fall of a house.' *And inextinguishable laughter rose among the gods.* My body convulsed at the thought of it. Suddenly a great convulsion twisted me again. My hand rose – the very grotto of the god! – and made the apotropaic sign. The dust and shattered leafage spilled and flew in a cloud. Some of it fell on the charcoal. There were bright sparks that seemed to dance over the surface. There were sudden small flames. There was smoke. It seemed to come at my face as if aimed like a weapon. I gasped in fear and got a lungful. I fell into a paroxysm of coughing. The whole cave or grotto grew immense and then contracted, seemed to diminish the movement into a pulsing. I heard a high note and then nothing.

I woke up, conscious of little but a headache. It was a long time before I dared to open my eyes. I was lying in the sumptuous bed of the First Lady. I turned my head and groaned at the pain of it. Ionides was sitting on the other side of the room. He stood up when he saw me move.

'Drink.'

I got myself up on one elbow. It was bitter-tasting stuff, willow bark I guessed, but almost at once my head cleared.

'What happened?'

'You very nearly started a fire, that's what happened. Enough smoke came out of the grotto for a volcano.'

'How did I get out?'

'I don't know. It's a strange place. There were people, attendants, moving about down there. I saw you carried sideways out of sight.'

'Where did they come from?'

'I told you the mountain has been excavated. They took care of the Pythia, that's all. I found you here.'

'The crowd –'

'They had the time of their lives, what with the laughter and the smoke. I only hope they will think it's holy, not comic.'

'The gods were there.'

'Gods?'

'Him. And him.'

'The fellow up the hill? Dionysus as well?'

'You heard them.'

'I heard you, that's what I heard. But still –'

'Ionides. What did the crowd hear?'

'Your two shouts first and that odd saying "One mouth or the other". Some sniggers. After that I gave our Roman guests their oracle. Then for a time you were mouthing. They all do it. Why can't the god do a clean job? Then it was the Athenian's turn, the official question of course, not the one about the corn and the Hellespont. I gave the answer we'd agreed on but you were still mouthing – mostly as far as I could hear you were mouthing about "lies and lees". That wouldn't do for an official party would it?'

'I suppose not. Ionides, did I really say things? I mean while I was what you call mouthing.'

'Of course you did. Like anyone else, there's no magic and nothing holy about it. It's just like any sleeper. After that came your little conflagration and those dark-clad attendants hauling you out. Don't worry. Nobody saw anything they shouldn't. We know about those things.'

'It's so mixed. I don't like it.'

110

'You aren't asked to like it. You'd better rest as much as you can. You're on again tomorrow.'

'But it's supposed to be one day!'

'Only two answers, the Romans and the Athenians? Oh yes, they're the most important of course. But we can't ignore the others, the whole crowd of them. After all, First Lady, it's how we get our living. It'll be little people mostly. You don't have to bother about them.'

'I don't want to bother about them!'

'Why do you suppose we had three Pythias? We were caught out this time by two so inconsiderately dying. But don't worry. Our spies are out. Well, not spies. Agents. The Athenians have a girl themselves and are putting her forward. Don't be surprised if you suddenly see a strange face.'

'A pretty one?'

'Are you remembering your Chloe? I don't know. Nobody tells me anything – I have to find it all out for myself. Well, I must go off and make friends with young Caesar, Julius. That young man asks too many questions for my comfort. By the way, the Athenian question will be slipped in among the small ones tomorrow. I mean the real one, the one that matters. I'm afraid we can't play about with that one.'

'We aren't playing about with anything! The gods were there!'

'Of course. If I can find anything out between now and then I'll let you know. But keep everything secret. They insist on your knowing nothing. They are really scared you see. So be a good girl and try to get the god to give an honest, divine opinion.'

'I am not liking this, Ionides.'

'You were highly recommended. But then so was that fat slug. Oh dear. This is life on a knife edge. It just occurs to me. Shall I ask you a question myself? One for me? My affairs? Slip it in among the others? After all I pass them on, don't I? Until tomorrow.'

There was a much smaller crowd next day. I passed through patches of silence in my vehicle and here and there could hear single voices or two in a conversation that ignored my passing. Judging by the sound of it the sacrifice was a she-goat who consented, poor female thing, as I was consenting, both used, both apparently prized for some quality but not rewarded for it except by – what? It was a question I was still asking myself as I was lifted down and set upright on the step. Going down in such a meditative mood, interspersed with no more than tremors of awe, I knew in some strange mood of certainty that the gods would deal gently with me this time. I was able to unwind my scarf calmly, blink and look about me and wait for the darkness to become no more than gloom. While I was waiting I became aware suddenly of the depth of the silence from the crowd outside. It was small indeed; yet there was no murmur from it, no single voice raised, not a cough or snuffle. They were there, each passion-

112

ately engaged to his question – perhaps life or death for them, wealth or poverty. First Lady, Pythia, is this pain in my side to continue increasing? How can I be healed? The doctor has given me up, First Lady. But she was an ordinary woman, not even a mother or a beauty, just a plain woman suffering the blight which the gods lay on her middle age.

The darkness was gone. I was seeing as in an evening light. The floor of the grotto was strange. There were lumps of worked stone here and there and in one place at least an iron bar stuck up from the stone and had been broken off. My Phocian ancestors, I thought to myself, this is where they found the treasure and tore it away from the stone, the nigh on life-sized statue of a woman in solid gold; one hundred and seventeen gold ingots each nine inches wide, three inches thick and eighteen inches long; mixing bowls, sprinklers, basins, a gold lion that had weighed nearly a quarter of a ton. Had that stone there, with leaded holes, held down the lion? Or were they so ignorant of man's greed that they would think the mere weight of the beast sufficient protection? And there were girdles and necklaces for the Pythia, were there not? But they would have gone early, passing as the Pythia passed, evanescent in the long run as raindrops. Well, thought I to myself, earnest people outside, you raindrops with your little worries, I will do what I can for you! I climbed carefully into the seat at the top of the tripod, seeing for the first time how the craftsman had combined seat and bowl, seeming to make the conjunction inevitable. And the legs of the brazier, their bronze was intricate with snakes and mice. Many hands had cared for this stone box of a grotto, and as I climbed into the seat, still facing it, I saw that at the back of the place a curtain hung. It made the flesh creep on my bones. Did that then hide the fabulous cleft in the rock up which once upon a time vapours had risen from the centre of the earth? It was with an effort that I turned my back on the curtain and settled in the seat.

There was much silence and at the end of it a touch of that same comedy which Ionides so much feared. He contributed it himself. There came a roll of timpani from out in the open air then silence again. I saw Ionides peering round the edge of his niche.

'I forgot to tell you. No shawms today.'

It was silly and made me laugh, not with the rollicking laughter of the gods but with my own voice, deep enough for a woman but not all that deep. Ionides began to pass on the questions one at a time. I forget what the first one was, but I found myself waiting for the god or gods and then talking to them. It seemed trivial enough. Here I am, I said, ready and willing. Do your will. Are you there? Both there, Dionysus, winter god for the three winter months, Apollo, you who mastered me yesterday, are you to do your will again? I am your Pythia.

There was no answer. Nothing. I thought to myself, long ago when they all turned their backs on me, I came to the void. Am I talking to it again? Apollo? Are you there?

Or are you away hunting up on Parnassus? Or chasing a laurel tree? Apollo, I believe in you. They want to know. Each one of them has brought you a gift. Will you answer?

Perhaps he put it in my mind, I don't know, but for the first time I thought of the dried leaves in the hollow flanges of the bowl. I took a pinch, noting as I did so that the flange had been refilled with a neat mound of the dusty stuff. I held it over the red moon of charcoal and let it sift and drift down from my fingers so that tiny sparks winked back at me and here and there a larger grain spurted with flame and smoke. It was pleasant enough, like throwing stones in water or playing at cup and ball. I did it again and seemed to do it again and again and again.

And again and again. But my hands were folded at my waist and on the coverlet of my bed.

'Apollo?'

There was no reply. I heard someone stir and thought it might be Dionysus. But Ionides answered.

'It is I. Good girl. Go back to sleep.'

But later that day I was, as Ionides had said 'on again'. I began to understand that he was passionately fond of dramatic representations, an art which has its own language, not just that spoken on the stage before an audience but spoken by actors when they are by themselves or accompanied by the technicians of presentation. I began to be concerned that in our dealing with the god or gods we were using a form of speech more appropriate to the modern kind of drama which, I am told, lacked dignity and religious feeling and had interest only in the mundane affairs of men. I began to understand by way of the language which Ionides used how the surroundings of the oracle had altered. I saw by the cramped nature of the building and the lack of provision for spectators that in times long past Delphi had been a far simpler place, perhaps no more than a village oracle. But Apollo had chosen it out of all the others, had slain the monster which guarded it and set up – however long ago – the circumstances which enabled the god's truth to be spoken here. Little by little its fame had spread and the authenticity of its words more and more credited as one after the other the words were seen always to enshrine truth. And we? We moderns? We had made a play of it, with scenery and a cast, with triviality, so that it became much as its new surrounds were. All that glitters was gold, except the words. I had spoken words and not known I had spoken them. They were the god's words.

Except those spoken by Ionides. It was with a sudden pang that I remembered. He had answered the two Romans out of his own head – and mine. The god had nothing to do with it. He should keep to his pigeons. He came back to fetch me.

'Ionides. We have blasphemed.'

'Yes.'

'You take it too calmly.'

'Almost anything we do concerned with gods is blasphemy if you must use that word. One god's truth is another god's blasphemy.'

'Don't be clever.'

'Good heavens, why not?'

'I was wanting to be reassured, that's all. I see you can't give it or won't.'

'But I've reassured you! Didn't you listen? I tell you what, First Lady, have a look at the take.'

'The what?'

'The take. The – remuneration. Those two Romans – oh my goodness! You should see the purse they left the Foundation and a necklace for you. Athens, dear, boring, traditional Athens, city of my heart for all her squads of professors, doctors, researchers, left a tripod, elegant enough and, I think, rather handed on as it were. Of course there was money for me but a bare minimum. We are none of us what we were. By the way they sent you another necklace. But don't worry about having too many. The First Lady – first slug – had an understanding with Leontes the goldsmith. He'll change anything into cash. Of course you can't go round selling things yourself.'

'The take.'

'Just so. By the way I haven't congratulated you – I do so now – on your performance yesterday. You were superb, my dear.'

'Yesterday? I didn't do anything!'

'Not anything? Not answering all those dim little people?'

'I went to sleep.'

'You seemed wide enough awake to me – just sufficient

touch of the, the "numinous" in your voice to carry complete conviction.'

'Numinous?'

'A word the Romans use. Means – spooky. Trust them, they're the most superstitious people in the world. God knows how they've got where they have. But when you answered the woman who wanted to know about her dead daughter the whole group of them started weeping. I very nearly did myself. How did you know that the child was called Lelia?'

'What child?'

'In any case, my dear, we have some completely satisfied customers. I'm not sure really that your "forte" doesn't lie in dealing with the simple rather than the complex! That woman took off her own earrings and added them to the drachmas. Not that they're much good – silver allegedly. Leontes will know.'

'I didn't know anything. I was asleep! Can't you believe me?'

'If you say so, of course. But if just sprinkling the stuff and then sniffing the smoke takes you that way I wonder how you'd have managed in the old days? The early Pythias used to chew the leaves, the fresh ones. If you'll notice, no animal eats laurel leaves, not even insects. They know. How I wish we did. But I think it's time you got ready.'

Ionides said he wished he knew but I don't think he did so wish. I was beginning to understand him. Most of his

118

mind was a kind of shell of opinions and brittle quips. Inside the shell was a mind made up and closed to change
because it was really a prime tenet of his that *he knew.*
In the shell itself were contrary opinions which he produced together with their opposites so that he was secure
from having to believe in any of them. I began to see how
the oracle, like Ionides, was surrounded by contradictions.
Whatever lay at the centre of the oracle, that mysterious
heart of it which spoke so often with riddling words so
that only a suppliant who was both wise and humble could
choose the right interpretation, I believed, no, I felt *I knew*
there was something connected with the hidden centre of
existence that lay there and sometimes spoke.

That day was the third day of oracular utterance, and
Ionides said he would have cancelled it had he known that
there would be only two suppliants and very bad weather.
It seemed foolish to go through all the outside ceremonial
– the wrapped Pythia, the festival vehicle which I had never
seen and the solemn ritual of the Descent. I recognized,
wrapped and blind though I was, that the vehicle was a different one and since I heard no onlookers in the street I
dared a look. I found I was riding in an ordinary, rather dirty
cart. There was one driver and one horse, hairy and slow.
That's right, I thought. That's how it must have been, back
in the old days just after the god had killed the monster. I
had a kind of joke with myself that one day this cart would
be all there was to take me to the cave and that the priest
of Apollo would have to drive it himself. But now the rain

was falling, beating on the great cloak they had thought to fold round my wrappings and I desired nothing so much as to get into the grotto out of the rain. At one point the horse stopped and staled there in the empty street and I came near to shouting at the driver. When we reached the portico it was Ionides himself who helped me down, murmuring as he did so, 'I can't lift you. You'll have to help yourself.'

So once inside I let the cloak fall, and could see the steps going down before me. I was wet, for all the cloak, and in a temper. I spoke sharply to Ionides, calling him Ion and asking him why he hadn't the wit to keep a Pythia dry and he answered that a Pythia with a god's help ought to be able to get out of a shower of rain. It was not edifying there on the steps going down to the oracle of the god. I became aware of this as I descended the wet and slippery steps and the god made me fall, which I deserved though he did nothing to Ionides who was as blameable as I. I thought of my father's words so long ago, 'In these cases my dear, it is almost always the girl's fault.' I had hurt my elbow, and stood in front of the tripod, rubbing the ache out of the bone. I suppose it was that hurt and the delay – let them wait! – that made me examine the curtain at the back of the grotto, though I went no nearer to it. I saw now that it was a representation of the fight between Apollo and the monster in what even I could see was intended to be the archaic manner. But what I had not noticed before was that there were two curtains side by side, drawn together by drawstrings. It only needed a pull on one of the strings to draw the curtains apart and reveal what they covered. I had a mind to go forward and solve a part of Apollo's mysteries. But as I debated that in my mind I heard Ionides' voice.

'Crates of Corinth – of *wealthy* Corinth – begs the god to tell him –'

I forget precisely what Crates wanted. What he got was an oracle given from Ionides' suddenly obsequious mouth which was mentioning large sums of money. The only other suppliant was a farmer whose farm was what he called 'sick' and what should he do about it? I began to feel we were very wicked. Ionides went up the steps, looked round in the street and then came back.

'All over. I'll call the cart back.'

It was in my mind to tell him not to bother and that I would walk. He and I might stroll out together, he with his sacred insignias over his arm, I with my scarf casually lying round my neck under a bare face, much as the performers of a marionette show will come out from the booth when the play is done and mingle with their own audience. It was, I said to myself, very nearly what the oracle had come to.

But then – there had always been the suspect and doubtful about the oracle even in the earliest recorded days. Those ancient hexameters – if the truth was to be told – were not really very good. As prophecy they were double-tongued, there was no doubt about that. Either the god would have his rollicking laughter, 'the fall of a house', or so subtle an interpretation that it might catch anyone. All that was agreed. No one expected the oracle to be anything else but riddling, and if you consulted it you took your chance that you could understand the real meaning of what the god said. But there was something else. The hexameters weren't very good yet Apollo was the god of the arts – of poetry! Why was his verse inferior to Homer's? Why was it that there were half a dozen poets who could create better verse than Apollo? Was there an answer to that? I thought back to my first awful meeting with the oracle, with the god, and how he had bloodied my mouth. Perhaps part of an utterance was always stained by the blood of the Pythia, unavoidably corrupted by her mortality so that the immortal god could only use her in her measure as a flute can only be used in its compass. It might, I thought, be that.

Ionides was waiting.

'I've called the cart. That Corinthian. Big business. We slipped up there –'

'And down there.'

'Yes. Were you hurt? We should have made more enquiries. I detected a certain sourness in him. He was annoyed at being in the third batch, as well he might. These big businessmen don't like waiting and he said so. I've had to ask him to supper at the palace of the Pythias.'

'Oh no!'

'You'll have to do it. This is Delphi, not some country town with nothing but hobbledehoys. A touch of mystery,

122

my dear. Do you think you could manage that?'

'I think we are downright wicked! I want to –'

Go. But where? Ionides was clever enough to understand exactly what I had not said.

'It's the sort of thing to mull over, dear First Lady. These occasions when things seem to tail off and become sordid are very trying. We live by the Great Occasions. You'll see. After all there's one every month. Isn't that enough for you? As for me – well, I suppose I am an old fraud – or you could say a really honest man who understands what he is doing and' – here he suddenly injected passion into the contrary argument and opinion – 'and realizes that the only thing that matters is the oracle, the oracle, the oracle! Preserve that and all is preserved.'

Delphi was strange. It had become a small town, almost deserted and dead in the three winter months – Dionysus was welcome to them – but bursting out of itself every month for the rest of the year. The numbers had declined steadily. About a third of the houses were empty except at the festivals, being reserved for visitors. Landowners from the surrounding country – but not my father, who preferred to cross the ferry to Corinth – had appropriated houses too big for smaller people and, in at least one case, an abandoned temple. It was these people and the family of the priests of those gods who were, dare I say, still alive, who were our society. We women were bare-faced. It was part of the civilization we shared with Athens from the old days. Some quite presentable

123

people were, I believe, glad they did not have to keep their women's faces covered in that it saved the cost of an expensive head-scarf. Our people, like all Hellas except a few favoured cities, knew poverty. I sometimes asked myself where it would all end and thought of asking Apollo on my own account, but by now knew too much about the oracle to believe the question worth asking him. I asked Ionides instead. It was at the dinner I gave for the big businessman. He had brought a woman with him, bare-faced and quite marvellously beautiful. I do not think she was his wife – or, at least, not his principal wife. There were also present Aristomachus and his wife Demareta. They were two of the local landowners I spoke of, though not the ones who had taken over a temple as a town house. Demareta was loquacious, something I was not yet used to in a woman. They truly *needed* a town house. Every year the countryside became more dangerous. Her husband told her she should not talk about such things but then, I noticed, said exactly the same thing himself and went on to explain it.

'The Macedonians, you see. They have to protect their borders and that should mean agreeing with Epirus. But all the mountains are full of brigands. I don't know, First Lady. Some are Illyrian, others from – well – even from Aetolia itself, and a whole rag-bag of creatures from anywhere and for whatever reasons! Every time the Macedonians carry out a sweep along their southern border we feel the effect of it from the increase in crime.

Now what I don't like is the way they've stopped fighting each other and are operating more or less wherever they like.'

It was the Corinthian who answered him.

'Have you complained to the Governor? For a Roman he's not bad. A present would be advisable but he'd send troops, perhaps even a punitive expedition. I know him as a matter of fact. I'll drop a word. After all he's always grumbling about his men down there in the Peloponnesus having nothing to do.'

Ionides pulled a face.

'Roman soldiers?'

'I see no harm in employing people according to their talent.'

'Meaning, my good sir, that Romans can fight whereas Hellenes and even Macedonians can't?'

'That's what it comes to. I'm a realist. A businessman has to be. It's all very well for priests and gentry to worship the old gods and have the daily work done for them, but business is different. When you said Roman soldiers in that snotty way – forgive me, ladies – you were acting the way that in business would lose you a fortune. You Greeks –'

'Aren't you a Greek?'

'Can't you tell from the way I speak? I'm a Phoenician. No, you Greeks can be brave, but mostly when fighting each other.'

Aristomachus flushed red. Perhaps it was his name coming out.

'I'm not sure that your opinion is as welcome as you are!'

It was my turn.

'But tell us about the Romans. We see so few of them here and they come as suppliants of course. Why are they so good at fighting?'

'Nobody knows,' said the Corinthian. 'For some reason they learnt in the dawn of time a lesson that we Hellenes have never learnt, not even in these modern days.'

The Corinthian's wife smiled sweetly at Ionides.

'Do tell us your thoughts, High Priest.'

'I can tell you what I think. An opinion. But I've no proof. It all stems from that bleeding head. When they founded Rome and began to build, they dug down on one of the seven hills and came on a freshly severed human head, still bleeding. The place is still called the Capitol which means, doesn't it, the place of the head? Well, if there's one thing you'd be if that happened to you, it's scared. Dead scared. Permanently, deeply scared. You see they aren't religious as we are, they're simply superstitious. Think of it! Finding a human head down there in the pit you've just dug and are still digging. A scared Roman is the most dangerous beast in the world. They began straight away, you see. They started wars with their neighbours – one little town fighting another – *because* if you don't push your neighbour a bit further away who knows what he might do? He has already – well someone has already planted a fearsome omen on you and who was nearest at the time, watching? So you either push him away or make him join you, ensuring at the same time that you've arranged that he agrees that you are top man. Only of course, after that, to be really sure, you have to be top man over your new neighbours who were once your neighbour's neighbours and so on. You end by pushing your fear all the way to the Red Sea in one direction and to Farthest Thule in the other! They'll have the lot before they've finished. It's fear that makes the heavens go round.'

'High Priest, you sound – I shouldn't say it – but you sound superstitious! "Fear makes the heavens go round!"'

'Well,' said the Corinthian, 'it doesn't make the world go round, that's for sure. But I come back to what I said. Why not employ people according to their talent?'

It was my turn again.

'But, good sir, you have not told us what was the lesson our Roman friends learnt in the dawn of time. Not to be afraid, surely!'

'Dear Lady, they learnt to combine. Just that. A legion is a single beast. Under a good general, and the gods know they have good generals, a dozen legions will become the separate arms of a single body – the general's body, if you will. They are indeed a dull lot, with a lust for slaughter which they satisfy at their festivals for the pleasure of men, women and children and call it religion. Everything in Rome is borrowed from you Greeks except, alas, the things that make them your masters.'

127

'Yours too.'

'Oh yes, High Priest. But we are a little people.'

The Phoenician big businessman turned then to Aristomachus.

'And you, sir, what do you think of our masters?'

'Meaning the Romans? If the Roman Governor can keep the peace on my uplands by crucifying a few outlaws and brigands I'll at least get something back for my taxes. As for the men themselves, I'm not like our Lady Pythia and His Holiness the High Priest of Apollo. I don't have to know them.'

'But you don't regret their rule? There's always a party in Athens – think of it! Shall I call it the "underground" party? – which wants Home Rule for Hellas. That's a fine thing to have scribbled on the walls of a cityful of professors – and on some of the finest walls too! Whoever they are they can't be real Athenians. They have no taste and can't spell. In fact, of course, under Roman rule Athens is actually a free city! But then, some people are never pleased with what they've got. If the Romans withdrew as they did not so long ago, Thebes would go through Athens as quick as boiled asparagus. Forgive me, First Lady. Your wine must come straight from Olympus. That sly child Ganymede must have been taking backhanders. It's nectar.'

'All the same,' said Ionides, 'you can understand them, young, and not seeing why foreigners who have no science, no religion, no philosophy, no astrology and no astronomy should be so important in their lives. Come, Aristomachus! You are as Hellene as any of us – more than most in fact. Wouldn't you agree to some slight feeling that a man should be his own master?'

'Who says I'm not?'

'Aristomachus dear,' said Demareta, 'remember what the physician said!'

'Drinking this nectar as somebody called it, you, I think, Your Grace, it's worth a bellyache or two. But don't say I'm not my own master or there'll be trouble!'

'You are as much your own master as any of us,' said Ionides, 'indeed sometimes –'

'We women are never free,' murmured the Phoenician's lady. 'It's rather nice really.'

I thought to myself, that man I was reading the other day, he was right. There are natural slaves. But I said nothing. The Corinthian evidently thought that it was his turn.

'I've travelled,' he said. 'That's as good an education as any. The conclusion I've come to in this matter of freedom is this. It's a question of size. What size group of people are we going to belong to? I don't think the gods have made us capable of rational judgement, which is where your philosophers go wrong. It's a man's instinct to belong to a group. Look at that fool Diogenes, thinking he was free when he had to beg his bread! Freedom isn't a simple thing because people make theories about it. The thing in itself, to coin a phrase, is not a matter of thought but a matter of feeling. If you are free where you voluntarily obey the local rules then you are as free as a man can be. But if your feelings won't stretch to a bigger entity, which makes the rules, then you don't feel free. As I see learning, I mean education, knowing what's what if you like, being street-wise – and for all your philosophers, that's what it comes to – is the ability to feel a larger entity. I sense that there's a feeling among you Greeks, an uneasy feeling, that you ought to feel for a huge area, I'll call it Panhellenia! Now. Can you feel for anything bigger than that?'

'You're confusing us,' said Aristomachus. 'We used to be a people of cities, and landowners such as I am always had town houses as well as country ones. You can't feel, really, for more than the city –'

'There you are, you see,' said the Phoenician. 'You believe in Panhellenia but you feel, really, for – what was your city, sir?'

'Phocis, I suppose. I haven't thought of it like that for years, though. My father had to sell the town house which is why we need one here.'

My turn once more.

'Aren't the Romans making what you, sir, called an entity? I should have thought that if you take the limits of the place where they rule it's the largest country in the world!'

'They have a phrase for it,' said Ionides. 'They call it *imperium romanum*, the Roman Empire.'

'Well there, you see,' said I, 'who on earth could feel for anything as dull-sounding as that?'

'Going round the world,' said the Phoenician, 'one comes across people who feel as we are saying, feel for the oddest groupings. But I've come to the conclusion that people would rather be ruled by a gangster of their own, however harsh his rule, than by a good and just ruler who is a foreigner. Don't ask me why. It's the nature of the beast. And so, with the greatest respect to you Greek gentlemen, I have to say that I don't believe you like Roman rule, and don't feel for the *imperium romanum*. What prevents you from scrawling Free Hellas or Free Panhellenica, or even Romans Go Home, on your walls is something so tenuous it would require only a hothead to set the country alight. Agreed?'

I signed to the slave for another round of drinks.

'It's lucky we have no Roman guests with us this evening. I don't think they'd be at all pleased.'

'Dear and revered Lady,' said Aristomachus, 'whoever would bother to tell them? Besides, Delphi is Delphi. Even the Romans acknowledge that we are the centre of the world.'

'All the same,' said Ionides, 'one ought to be clear that our cases are hypothetical. We are none of us free. We don't, despite Pythagoras, choose to be born or choose to die. It is only the Alexanders who to some extent control their fate. Indeed,' and here he turned and smiled at me, 'I remember once telling our First Lady that on occasion she is free and in fact is the only really free person in the world.'

'Oh no, Ionides, not free! But it is not fitting to say more on that subject. You have travelled, sir. Have you found a fairer country than Greece?'

'Fairer countries enough, Lady, but never fairer women.'

There was a murmur of agreement from the men and the Corinthian's woman bridled and simpered. I, alas, had no cause to do either.

'So,' said the Corinthian, 'we are agreed are we not that the Roman rule is to be borne?'

'What,' said Ionides softly, 'what could we do about it if we don't?'

'Nothing,' said Aristomachus.

'Nothing,' said the Corinthian.

'All the same,' said Ionides, 'there is that quote underground unquote party in Athens. You, sir, who have travelled so much – have you not heard of the same in other Hellenic cities?'

The Phoenician peered at him over his cup.

'Just exactly why do you want to know?'

'You, sir, are a foreigner. You can say things we might – hesitate to say.'

'I have heard it said. I have seen this scrawl and that, here and there.'

'What does the Governor think?'

'Why should he think anything? Hellas is at peace.'

'Except for the brigands,' said Aristomachus.

'Except for the pirates,' said Ionides.

The Corinthian's wife turned to him.

'Do tell us about the pirates!'

'Just that it's becoming unsafe to travel anywhere by sea at this end of the Mediterranean. The Romans keep the waters between us and them, little more. In the old days your country had the eastern half of the sea in their charge but not any more. You can't afford it.'

There was then a long discussion of piracy and I was grateful, for I was tired and did not want to listen to anything or do anything but go to sleep. I heard with half an ear the Phoenician explaining how when he had 'first started' all you had to fear was the odd ship, sometimes no more than a pulling boat with three pairs of oars which they had to ship before they could board you. Sometimes, he said, you could get them to stay in their boat while you paid them off. It was a kind of toll, really. But then it got worse, cut-throats and in caiques under sail, smart craft that could outsail anything but a trireme. But now it was the pirates that had the triremes and sometimes a whole fleet of them, sweeping a stretch of sea, as it might be the western shore along past Smyrna, and gobbling and sinking anything in sight. Governments? The local governments didn't do anything – hadn't the money or should we say the financial resources, not even Delos or Rhodes. It would come to the Romans, that would be it. Not natural sailors at all but they could learn and did, as the Carthaginians learnt to their cost.

133

VI

It would be wearisome to recount the monthly festivals of the oracle and my descent into the grotto, once so feared and never entirely discounted. I did sometimes give an answer in hexameters though that was never easy. It required a certain elevation of the spirit though it caused a greater stir than I was aware of at the time. The fact was that this kind of versified answer had not been used for generations. When the news reached Athens that the Pythia was using Apollo's own language again, if only now and then, there was a whole new reason for visiting the oracle. Presently Ionides began to limit his own emendations and gave the enquirers what I had said straight. I was flattered by this and indeed I still think some of the answers were felicitous but I shall not repeat them. Ionides did on several occasions threaten to 'publish' them in a book. There are a number of collections of our sayings — not mine, the oracle's — which I suppose you could say had been 'published' through the generations, though the Foundation was in possession of the only copies and did not allow unauthorized perusal. That was what Perseus said, 'unauthorized perusal'. I don't know why I found the phrase so funny and used it so often that Ionides remarked I was becoming a bore. I found after my first terrifying descent into the grotto that I still felt the awe one finds on entering a temple or even when standing before it in a state of what the Foundation calls 'recollection'. It seemed to me that after his first – I shall dare to call it 'rape' of me, that he had thought that enough was enough, and broken in as I was I could now be ridden with the gentlest of touches. It made me understand that play of Euripides better than the poet himself had done! Indeed, when I saw it – for I had to sit by the priest of Dionysus at the dramatic representations – I wept behind my veilings and could not tell whether it was in joy or sorrow. These are mysteries. It may be, as Ionides used to say in his really cynical days, that all these old legends do not conceal and shadow forth profound religious truths but rather they state bluntly the great human truths which may be as valuable. But I think Ionides was changing. I detected in what he said sometimes the suggestion that all religions were not foolish nor their customs, and that the cosmos which we inhabited was a stranger place than people sometimes thought. We must not, he once said, take our modern wisdom for granted as a final thing.

After the festival of that first month I was astonished not just by the number of presents left for me but by their variety. I have said, I think, how rich were those left by the two young Romans. But the others ranged all the way down, if that is the right direction, to some vegetables and a dead hare. As the months revolved and Ionides took jewellery to the goldsmith on my behalf I found myself rapidly becoming a wealthy woman in my own right. Now I understood why the apartments of the First Lady held a cupboard which locked, a modern chest which locked, and, most interestingly, a very, very ancient chest which screamed rather than creaked when I opened it. Ionides swore he had never seen it before and we opened it with some, shall I say, holy trepidation; for even the apartments of the Pythias had something of the grotto about them. However, scream or not, we got the box open between us and it held nothing but some bricks. They had queer signs on them which made Ionides cry out. They were the same as the Cretans had used in old times. He sent for Perseus who read them for us. He said it was a list of things and it would be reasonable to believe that the list was of what the chest had once contained; gold ingots, if that was to be believed, and images and a censer. Perseus stopped in the middle and went red in the face and I thought he would fall into an apoplexy but he did not. Instead he burst out with a kind of gasping speech. 'Don't you understand? Gold ingots! This was part of the treasure which Croesus sent to the oracle. You remember – there were girdles and necklaces for the Pythia and obviously she had an ingot or two. That is' – and it was quaint to see how the words written on the bricks had made him feel for a moment that the gold was really still there! – 'she did have an ingot or two. The writing is the one used by the Hittites. This is all, oh, six or seven hundred years old – unimaginable!'

I had never seen our friend Perseus so elevated. It was touching, for indeed there was no gold to be seen, but what Plato, perhaps, would call the IDEA of gold. Ionides called it that with some bitterness when he had recovered from the excitement of opening the chest with its iron bands and locks and corner pieces. He recovered himself by giving us a short lecture on the Hittites, how they discovered iron and conquered right down into Egypt because their weapons were practically modern. Ionides, I am afraid, is a typical Athenian of our times, that is to say, he is a professor. But when we had thrown away the bricks with their odd signs, dusted the chest inside and oiled the hinges, it became a fine receptacle for the money which Ionides brought back to me after his forays to the goldsmiths. I ought to add that when we found the chest the ancient key was still in the lock. But it broke after a few attempts at using it and we had to get a locksmith to make us a new one. So there I was, a woman with a fortune and no one to give it to. Nor could I spend it really, for the apartment of the First Lady was almost too full of rich things which Ionides said did not belong to the Pythia 'but,' said he, smiling his sad smile, 'to the IDEA of the Pythia of which, my dear, you are an individual copy!'

'And all this in the chest?'

'That is yours. No one would doubt it. After all,

everytime they give you a present they give me one. If yours isn'tyours then – you see?'

As far as people outside Delphi were concerned I began to understand the extraordinary nature of their belief in me. If it comes to that, belief in any Pythia! But it was as if in their mind there was one Pythia and that the original one. They might hear – and did – that there were three Ladies, as when I came to the oracle. They heard, they understood and yet they believed in the one Pythia! They had heard that two of the three Ladies had died, but somehow the news was mysteriously adapted to what they felt. If two women had died, well it meant that She, the Pythia, had not died – I cannot explain it because I never understood the transaction myself. What of myself? The ordinary – let us say – Athenian may have had his belief in the Pythia easily reconciled with its illogic because he only thought about the question a few times in his life, and notably if he had a question to ask. But I – how did I view myself? Did I believe in what I was doing? Or rather, since I was doing nothing, did I believe in what someone, something was doing to me? Women are sometimes hysterical and do and say the strangest things. But that remark is going to circle round and bite its own tail – perhaps the truth of life and living lies in the strange things women do and say when they are hysterical. Perhaps the first time I went shrouded down the steps as into my own grave I became hysterical. A medical condition. Or possessed by a god. By him. Him. It was something

I brooded over. I made up my mind quite soon that the reasonable thing to do was to sacrifice to Apollo regularly. To talk to him when I chose to. If he objected to the impertinence of this approach he had every means at his disposal for making his disapproval known. There had been a brutality in his rape of me or in my hysteria. He, after all, had put me in a certain position. He owed me something: a tricky statement to make where a god may be listening! The unasked-for response might be painful – infinitely painful! But one comes to a place. Yes. It is a dry and dusty place where unease and doubts have blown about until that wind drops and they fall in unswept heaps. Yes. It is a place. The risk of that painful answer recedes. Are you there, sir? Once, you turned your back on me or I turned your back for you. God, god, god. I could call out in hexameters, in Latin, in Hittite, what difference would it make? Oh, my soul, how shall I keep silent? Ah ha, you recognize that do you not? The raped Creusa raging against the god who had raped her and begotten Ion to be priest of his temple.

They performed that, just up the hill. I was there, as I said, with the Priest of Dionysus on one side of me and Ionides the Priest of Apollo on the other. No man understands what rape is. No one there did. The argument does not even bite its own tail but goes on circling. We pretty it up. Ionides told me beforehand what the argument of the play was, my first play, he showed it to me in writing in the bookroom but it was not like that. I knew what she

142

meant. How shall I make it plain? He tore her. He tore my entrails and bloodied my mouth. Hysterical women.

So there we were, with time marching on downhill. There were the Delphian games of course, running and jumping. All for the god and the prizes. It's the tourist trade which pays for the prizes really, though they're like everything else, not what they were. I had to put in an appearance and have never been so bored in my life. When the runners came up for their prizes full-frontally I didn't know where to look. However it really was good for business and if Delphi looks prosperous every month when the Lady is giving out the Good Word, during the games when she is silent the place is booming. You would think buying and selling would never cease. Then, of course, winter comes. Officially – or have I said this? – it's all over to Dionysus. Actually, Delphi dies on its feet. The place really is dead. We locals dine with each other and pretend we are just as civilized as Athenians but we can't ever quite get over the sense that we're not fashionable, we're holy. That takes the top layer off party conversation. Forgive a frivolous old woman.

Astonishingly enough it was Ionides who defined my status for me.

'My dear Arieka' – for when no one else was about he sometimes did address me by my given name – 'there is not a woman in the district of Delphi who would dare to refuse an invitation from the First Lady! Indeed, we could increase that area. There's no woman, not in Megara,

possibly in Thebes and *certainly* not in Corinth where all
being deep in trade they positively worship any institution older than yesterday – you'd have them across in your
father's ferry in swarms if you just crook your little finger.
Shall you?'

'Why?'

'It would break up a little bit of the dreary winter.
Besides – besides, it would help me.'

'Would you care to explain.'

'Oh dear. I don't think I ought. On the other hand – let's
say it would help me, speaking as a pigeon fancier.'

'You talk about information gathering. In the whole of
this last season I can't remember a question in which what
you know about the world helped or affected the answer.'

'You wound me.'

'I'm sorry.'

'No. I don't want you to change. You're too honest.'

'Oh if you only knew!'

'Doubts? We all have them. I wasn't meaning that. I
was meaning your attitude to the whole situation. You
don't see what's happening.'

'I don't have to.'

'The Romans.'

'The pirates.'

'The brigands.'

'The god doesn't seem interested.'

'There you are, you see. You are indeed too honest. You
are restricting the god to looking for stray sheep or find-

ing someone's grandmother's necklace for them.'

'It's what I'm asked.'

'Arieka – First Lady – can't you compel the god?'

'I've never heard of such a thing! I'm not sure –'

'Wait. Have you read Theocritus?'

'Some.'

'Simaetha?'

'The girl who wants her lover back? Oh, Ionides! What blasphemy!'

'Of course I don't mean magic. But somehow the god's answers seem to lack a certain universality.'

'The fault, dear Ion, is not in the god.'

'But the questions?'

'Yes.'

'I wonder what the world would say if it overheard us? Shall I tell you the truth of our situation?'

'It sounds dangerous.'

'It is. You are asking me to rig the questions and I am asking you to rig the answers.'

'I think you'd better go.'

'No. Consider.'

'No.'

'Consider. I shan't ask you again.'

It was true the god had raped me. It was also true that earlier he had turned his back on me and now seemed to be doing much the same.

'I can't, Ion. It's not a question of fearing the consequences. It's because – I don't know what.'

VII

That night after he had gone, I tried to be a philosopher without knowing how. It was the gods. Ion said they have a new god in Egypt, one the philosophers have put together out of the remains of three old gods. I made a note in my mind to ask Ion the name of the god and he told me it was Serapis. But that must be wrong. The trouble with the old gods is that if you put them together they fight. After all, the conduct of Ares and Aphrodite on the windy plain was unbecoming. You can't get anywhere by making a bunch of gods because you're looking in two directions at once and stuck. At some point in my thoughts I remembered how the gods had turned – but at that length of time, remembering, things change. They had turned their backs on me – or had I turned their backs for them, as for example if you have a small image of your favourite god you sometimes turn it facing away because it can't see what you're doing. Which would imply that, even as a girl, I hadn't really had much belief – no, much *use* for the Olympians. So that void which I felt I had come across and before which I lay in grief was – a kind of god? No. A void is a void, a nothingness. My hair prickled and I felt as though the skin of my back had frozen. I was an unbeliever. I was anathema. Swiftly I rearranged my thoughts until they became acceptable – Zeus the Father of men and gods, Artemis the merciless one, Hera the jealous wife, which is why all wives as far as I can see are jealous – or contrariwise. I wish, indeed I wish, I had been a boy: not for the freedom of going anywhere but for the freedom of thinking anything, following any thought to where it ought to lead if that is what logic is. I said to myself, ask Ion. How like a woman! But I was unlike women in this, that I did not believe Ion, or only some of the time. What did Ion believe in? Very little, if anything, and it changed as he spoke, following words towards a cleverness. Anything for a laugh. But *not* the Olympians when considered as a Greek thing. Oh yes! In the time I had known him Ion had changed. In the early days he had daringly allowed me to see that he did not believe even in the All Father. But he would not allow this to be seen among foreigners – barbarians – because that diminished his real love, which I had found more and more was simply Hellas herself, the Greek thing, that thunderous roll of names from the early days, the like of which is nowhere else on earth. But of recent days it had seemed to me that perhaps he had come to believe a little and think, even, that being a priest as he was was something real. So no Ion or no questions from me that might disturb his tired, his ageing approach to the mystery. Let him continue to believe that, despite the Romans, one day Greece, Hellas, would be herself again.

If not Ion, then who? There was only one answer. The god. Ask the oracle on your own behalf! Ask the oracle if it existed? What nonsense was that? A paradox, was that what they would call it? The void then. And the hexameters. And now and then the oracle had seemed to work. Mostly it was what Ion called the Escape Clause. There was always something in the answer which could be interpreted in different ways. Even if I was too positive, Ion's transmission of the words would alter them subtly, toning down the positive and implying an alternative. Oh yes! Between us we were clever. And sometimes we were lucky. If you add the occasional luck to the information service which Ion's pigeon post shared with all the other oracles, from Siwa to the oracle in the Cassiterides at the North Pole, we were occasionally very lucky indeed. But never as lucky as Croesus with his lamb and his tortoise in a bronze pot! Also the questions were fewer and smaller. So were the presents. We had declined from gold, via the Athenian drachma, to silver. Sometimes we received nothing but a letter of thanks. Sometimes we did not even get that. However, this was Delphi and her riches were legendary. Ion remarked one day that the roof of the hall of the Pythias – the Pythion – needed looking at. The next thing I knew he had a quite famous Athenian architect crawling round on the tiles. Andocides was small, hairy and irreligious.

He referred to our temples as 'god boxes' and the treasuries as 'money boxes'. I don't know how he referred to me behind my back but to my face he was civil enough, even though I was now accustomed to go about with my face bared. After all he was an Athenian where anything goes except dullness. But he was abrupt.

'You'll have to move out.'

I looked at Ion.

'It can't be as bad as that.'

'It is,' said Andocides. 'Even Mycenaean work doesn't last for ever. This place must be a thousand years old. The lead is eaten to pieces and half the stonework worn through.'

'Can't it just be left as it is?'

'Yes,' said Andocides sourly, 'if the Lady doesn't mind the whole thing falling on her head next winter.'

'Where can I go?'

'I'm your guardian,' said Ion, 'you could move in with me at a pinch.'

'I've seen a number of houses here empty,' said Andocides. 'If I'm going to be here long enough to oversee the repair of the roof I'll need a house.'

'Take your pick,' said Ion. 'They're abandoned and falling down most of them. You might be lucky.'

Andocides did set up a temporary home in one of the houses, a very small one. But most of his time he spent on the roof. Then he came down and asked to see us both. He wasted no words.

'The roof must come off and be rebuilt. And quickly. In my view you don't even have time to wait for summer. It's a chancy business.'

'Can't you shore it up for the time being?'

'What! At that height? Where are the trees?'

'Have you any idea of the cost?'

'I could give you an estimate.'

'Please. As soon as possible.'

'I've been thinking about it up there. I can give you a rough estimate here and now, provided you won't hold me to it.'

'Speak.'

Andocides told us. The sum meant little to me. Above a thousand drachmas sums have always seemed the same to me and meaningless. But Ion sat down so carefully I knew he was avoiding doing it with a bump.

'As much as that?'

'I think so. That's leaving nothing for myself. Call it an offering to the god.'

'But you're notorious – an atheist!'

'I can't see a fine old building like this fall into a heap of rubble.'

'We are in a fix,' said Ion. 'You know we haven't money like that here. I shall have to go to Athens and beg.'

'Try Corinth. That's where the money is.'

'I'm an Athenian,' said Ion stiffly. 'Athens shall have first chance. After all, this is Delphi and all the world will contribute.'

'The sooner you let me know the better,' said Ando-cides. 'I'll do what shoring I can in the winter. But with spring the roof must come off.'

'Can't I do anything, Ion? You know I have some –'

Andocides laughed.

'Ask the god for a fine winter, Lady,' he said. 'If he gives us a bad one the weight of snow on a roof of that pitch – perhaps the weather was better in the early days. Well. I'll leave you, look at the figures and give you a written estim-ate. High Priest, Lady –'

'I don't think I can stand up,' said Ion. 'To think of the time we've spent under this roof without even thinking of it!'

'Ion.'

'What is it?'

'You are going to Athens this winter.'

'It would seem so.'

'Why can't I come too?'

'My dear Arieka!'

'There's no reason why not. Dionysus will look after the oracle during the winter. He always does and nobody bothers him with questions. Please!'

'Dear First Lady, what would we do? Think of the, the scandal.'

'That's foolish. I'm an old woman. Besides, if necessary we can stay in different places. I would like to travel just once in my life.'

'I don't know.'

'Think about it – please!'

'Are you a good beggar? That's what we should have to be, you know. A million drachmas! Do you know what that means?'

'You are going to talk about numbers and give me a headache. I think I could be a beggar – perhaps a good beggar. I'd try.'

'I'll think.'

'Is Delphi really as famous as we claim?'

'Yes. Yes of course. It's known from Stonehenge to Aswan. Probably further still by the will of the gods.'

It was on the tip of my tongue to say that he used not to believe that the gods had any will at all. But I decided to keep quiet.

Next day Ion said he thought it might be possible for me to go. He had sent a message and the answer was not unfavourable. Athens, or Ion's contact in Athens, needed a few days to arrange things. Then there might be an official invitation. He guessed that nobody quite knew how to receive a Pythia or even if it was, so to say, theologically possible. A Pythia and Delphi in the common mind were one and the same thing and that might be that: in which case I should spend yet another three months of seclusion in a snowed-up village.

Two days later Ion said that the answer was a definite yes. Athens, in fact, had thought about it and said the possibilities were simply marvellous! It had never happened before. They were about to send messages in every direction saying that the oracle was coming to Athens and in the tourist season! They calculated on an absolute flood of Romans, let alone Greeks from the East and Egypt. They were arranging a pomp to bring me in and up to the Acropolis and the temple of Pallas. Ion, of course, would be staying with Apollo in his own Athenian temple.

The last month of summer wore on. It seemed to me that there were fewer people about than usual. We were to meet our conductors at my father's house down by the sea and I was to travel in the vehicle I had never seen! Ion and I came as near a real quarrel over that as we ever had. I was determined to inspect the vehicle. It was one thing to be moved, shrouded and alone, in some kind of cart for a hundred yards or so. It was quite another to go down that steep hill up which I had been brought so many years ago, and then, if I survived that, to be driven all those miles to Athens. In the end I got my way. The vehicle was wheeled out of one of those Delphian secret or at least secluded buildings with well-locked doors and brought to the hall of the Pythias for my inspection. It was a very interesting object. It had four wheels, and the front two, together with the shafts, could move a little from side to side. It was very big and painted all over. There was nothing of Apollo about it whatsoever and I guessed that it had been made in the days before Apollo took over the cave and the oracle. I say it was 'made' in those days; but quite clearly, to anyone who knew anything about farming, it had been repaired a hundred times over. But I also guessed that the painting had been reproduced each time as nearly as possible. So, plain to see was the picture of the python in the cave, the python which Apollo would one day kill, and also our fat Mother Gaia. But from my point of view the cart, for that is what it really was, had been well looked after and I might trust myself to it – indeed it had been better maintained than the hall of the Pythias! I allowed little Menesthia to stand in as the oracle of Dionysus. I said she was not to go into the cave but might sit under the portico and answer any questions there might be. She was a strange child and had some way of deliberately making herself, as she said, 'feel funny' and she would do that and answer the question. She also said she would examine the enquirer's palm because you could tell a lot about his future that way. I asked her if she had ever divined by means of water in a pot. She said no, her mother used to but said it was dangerous. So I was sure the oracle, in so far as it affected Dionysus, was in interesting hands, even if they were not necessarily oracular.

I cannot say that visiting my father's old house was very affecting. My brother who had inherited was away – but then he was always away and we should not have recognized each other. His wife was there, fat and frightened of the Pythia I was glad to see, not having ever connected that house with anything but little put-upon Arieka. It was one of the few times I ever really enjoyed the prerogatives of my position. Ion was not so happy and insisted on our spending the night at the house because he had walked down with his horse led by a slave and his feet were sore. Besides, the pomp had not yet arrived. It was coming by ferry and was stuck in Corinth.

Next morning it arrived and we set off. I must say I think I should have felt safer had we gone via Megara rather than across the ferry; but Megara and Athens at that time were having one of their endless tiffs. It never got so far now that we were subject allies of the Romans, and a Pythia is quite as sacred as the image of a god. No one without the insolence of an Alcibiades would mistreat a divine image! But the Megarans were uneasy, which is why we and our pomp crossed by ferry to Corinth.

To see a city across water, and certainly Corinth, was magnificent enough. But those buildings, which I in my childhood had taken as the dwellings of the gods, were warehouses built along by the water! Here we were received by our Corinthian friend who was to entertain us. His house, or palace rather, was gross. Nevertheless it was comfortable and guarded by Roman soldiers. Since they burnt Corinth down they have not been popular. Nor have their friends – among whom was ours – and there was a rowdy element in the city. Ionides startled me by saying they were the salt of the earth and I had to question him several times to be sure that he meant what he said. This was a seed blown by the wind that might lodge anywhere. But I do not concern myself with the internal organization of cities. Suffice it to say that our friend contributed handsomely to the fund for the roof of the Pythion. After only one night we proceeded on our way, a long day's journey, and arrived at Eleusis after dark amid the flare of torches. We stayed here two nights and I must not say much about it. I was greeted with reverence by the mystai and granted certain privileges which I shall not specify, though initiates may well guess what they were and are. Yet I was, in a certain way, disappointed. Delphi and Eleusis are the right and left hand of the god. Or perhaps it would be better to say that while Delphi is the voice of a god, Eleusis is the god's hands! But I do not specify in these matters. On the second morning after the kiss of peace we went on to Athens.

Those who have never seen Athens should rest easy. She is as she is claimed to be. There is a whole population of statuary which the Romans have not touched. Athens is a free city, they have declared so, I mean the Romans, in their Senate. Her citizens can carry arms if they want to, though as far as I can see very few avail themselves of the privilege. There are many slaves in the city and many freed men. Women of the better sort go nearly enough bare-faced like us Delphians. We seemed, however, to meet only philosophers and professors and of course writers and poets, though just at the moment they have no one outstanding. They are careful of their speech so that in some ways it sounds old-fashioned.

Once more we were greeted with courtesy and awe. I do not believe the awe was deeply felt. It seemed more as if these reverend gentlemen were displaying a form of what they thought they ought to be feeling. I had in sudden shyness rather than modesty veiled myself completely.

It was, however, something of a shock to find that one was to be housed in the Parthenon and in rooms partitioned off behind the colossal image of the goddess herself. When you consider that the Winged Victory she holds in her right hand is life-size you get some idea of how appallingly bad the statue is. To begin with there is no point from which it may be seen standing as it were, at ease. Because the head is right up there it looks too small, and the hand down here is so much larger than life it is gross. The whole sacred image does not give an impression of the holiness and power of the goddess but of the sedulous scurrying of the ants who put her body together. The spear that lies in the crook of her left arm is larger than the mast of a trireme. No Athenian I spoke to admired it. They would draw me to one side and bid me admire some elegant and gesticulating confection in which the stone-carver had achieved impossibilities of representation and complexity. But often I found the colours too bright, being more used to the ancient images of Delphi where time had often dimmed the colours back to what must have been something like the unadorned stone. The paintings in the stoas were another matter. Here you could feel yourself actually present at the siege and burning of Ilium. You could gaze into the furious face of Ajax and admire the hale old age of Nestor.

But I am indulging myself in the memory of my travels. After all, this was the first time I had moved more than a few miles from the house where I was born and I do not expect ever to travel again. For where is there to go? I have seen Athens and live in Delphi! But it is time I got on.

We were entertained at banquets. The ladies lay on couches instead of sitting up on chairs and were bare-faced, much as we women are at Delphi. One feels oneself part of an advanced civilization. I, of course, in view of my position occasionally drew my scarf across my mouth, but I think the ladies found this an appropriate and deli-cate reminder. Even the Archon's wife. At some point in these banquets – except the utterly exclusive ones – Ionides would speak. This was done in the Athenian way as if by accident. Someone would refer in the course of his remarks to the time his grandfather had consulted the or-acle and how impressed he had been by this or that. Then would follow a direct question to Ionides about people he had met at Delphi, which would enable Ionides to give his reminiscences of Sulla the Roman dictator and how he had laughed at the decay of the buildings, saying that Greeks could build but not maintain. And so to the fact that our roof was in danger of falling in. Once a wit in-terjected at this point, 'My Dear High Priest, Aeschylus was wise after all!' When that ice had been broken a far too good-looking young woman – I think she was one of those whom we call hetaeras – confessed that she had

161

wanted to address me but did not dare, because everybody was simply bursting with curiosity to know *what it was like*. This daring approach would start a truly Athenian conversation, a kind of cross talk of allusions and witty remarks which a stranger would not understand – I did not – but the gods were bandied about. I have lost my thread. These conversations were what I can only call delicately blasphemous. Indeed, one young man with what I can only call a laughing raillery accused Ionides of inventing the prophecies himself. This brought a sudden and, I really believe, shocked, silence. Ionides lied calmly.

'I have never made up an oracle. We are, I think, going too far in our discussion of oracular inspiration, in view of what and who is sitting veiled and silent among us. But let me say I have always passed on what I heard, and where I was uncertain of what I heard I have said nothing. You know that the oracle has sometimes returned to the ancient custom of speaking in hexameters again. I am a channel only. I am no poet and could not invent these verses myself. They come from a mouth that is pure and holy and the god speaks through it.'

The silence was prolonged. It was in my mind to accuse Ionides of the ultimate blasphemy in his claim. But I did not. How could I? But there was more that kept me silent. Here was the atheist speaking: and I knew him well enough to know that he was speaking in all sincerity. He believed what he said, or I knew nothing about him. So Ionides, cynic, atheist, contriver, liar, believed in god!

I suppose we all change. I had believed in the Olympians, all twelve of them. How much did I believe now, after years of hearing Ionides inventing speeches for me? How much after years of inventing them myself? How much after years of remembering that the god had raped me, years of part-belief, of searching for a proof that all I had believed in was a living fact and if twelve gods did not live on that mountain, they did in fact, in real fact, live somewhere, in some other mode, on a far greater mountain? It was too much for me. I did not speak out but kept silent, veiling my head completely.

Ionides thought this a calculated gesture. But I did it in sheer shame.

He went on, and before I had returned to listening apparently he had managed to turn the awkward corner from religious awe to the respect due to wealth. Yes, he was saying, it was a fact that the oracle was reduced to – not to put too fine a point on it – to begging! He had not thought of boring this distinguished company with sordid financial and well, simply financial affairs! Of course if anyone wished –

Yes, they did wish. The Archon called for his stylus and tablets and wrote down a sum. The rest promised. Women proposed gifts of jewellery. It was clear that Athens for all she wore no weapons still had her resources.

'Tourism mainly,' said Ionides on the way back across the Field of Mars. 'Also the university. Athens isn't much else but a university these days. That's a lot of course.'

'It looks like a stonemason's yard. All these gesticulating heroes and clean, bare altars!'

'Which reminds me. Dear First Lady, could you not contrive sometimes at these beanfeasts – did you hear the Archon? – could you not contrive to be a little more . . . *mantic*? Of course I know you *are*, but these people have to be reminded constantly that Delphi is a *living oracle* and vital to the well-being of the country and the world.'

'Is it?'

'I appreciate that you're tired. But remember the roof!'

By the time we had been ten days in Athens I was beginning to understand the reality of things Athenian. Her professors were exquisite even in their eccentricity. I had never felt myself surrounded by such a mild and amused warmth of respect and understanding. Their students were courteous. A great many of these were Romans sent to Athens to perfect their education. Some of them were more Greek than the Greeks, just as some of the Greeks, I am ashamed to say, played at being Roman. We moved in the highest ranks of society and never came near getting our million drachmas. We received genuine respect, some perhaps genuine belief, a great many protestations of affection, and very little money.

Ionides grew increasingly bitter. He was forever consulting a small roll on which he had set down the various sums already donated. One day he wished to reckon what sum they came to when put together. He was a long time about it and confessed at last that he kept getting different totals. He asked a professor of mathematics to help him, having found out that I was unable to.

'My dear fellow,' said the professor, 'you should ask a shopkeeper. He'd do it in a flash on his abacus.'

But Ionides insisted, not wishing to make the smallness of our donations too obvious. So the professor did what he called adding them up. He had a simple method of counting in fives, tens and scores, and after perhaps an hour by the waterclock he achieved a result.

'We call it counting on our fingers and toes,' he said.

When Ionides saw the total he was silent for a while. The professor seemed about to make a further comment but changed his mind, and after thanking him we left. Ionides was moody.

'This won't go far,' he said. 'I don't know what we can do. Dionysus is our last chance.'

It was not only our last chance but our last engagement in Athens. We were to go in procession to his altar and sacrifice there.

The procession was a small one but the crowds were big. It was really the first time I had realized that the townspeople were of a different sort. There were not many slaves. Athens prefers freed men. I suppose it is an advance in civilization. Though over this question of slavery I have a confused mind. I remember Perseus in the bookroom, happy in his work and regarding 'freedom' with grave mistrust. After all, if slavery is the limitation of freedom certainly there are real slaves in mines for example. But there are men who have to plough, dragging the plough themselves since they have no oxen. What I am looking for is a phrase, if I can remember it, which Ionides gave me. Yes, I remember. It is a question of degree. There is employment of one man by another. This varies right through from abject slavery to – in the case of Perseus – a chosen and enjoyed wedding between the man and his work. You could in any case say that we are all slaves of the gods or the idea of the gods, or subject, if it comes to that, to the law. Limitation is a fact of life. Yes, I am muddled. Once Ionides said 'When you are sitting on the tripod you are the freest being in the world.' Did I say that when he said it I burst into tears and did not know why? I do now. I was the slave of god or the idea of god. You see how learned I have become with all my reading in the bookroom! Yes, it is Plato's, this idea.

The procession to the temple of Dionysus was at once a triumph and a disaster. As soon as our procession appeared a man shouted 'There she is!' A woman screamed and fell down. Then the crowd fell into a foaming frenzy – this sophisticated Athenian crowd, at the sight of a veiled woman, went mad. The tall police with their clubs closed round us and beat them off, but I believe we were in much peril of being crushed to death. I had never before appreciated disciplined men. They were wholly brutal in a matter-of-fact way. If a skull needed to be cracked it was cracked. If moving forward meant stepping on fallen bodies then these heavy men with their clubs and shields, their blank and vizored helmets, trod on them: and, borne where they wanted us to go, we must perforce step on crushed and bloodied bodies, too. We never reached the temple but returned whence we came. The bodies lay for a while where they had fallen because the dull sky let down snow. The priest of Dionysus, I later heard, had viewed the bodies and declared that the sacrifice had been made. But by then we were on our way home.

I have to say that, even taking the inclement weather into account, our departure was less splendid than our arrival. The departing guests were not so much sped as ignored. It was a small body of police that escorted us to the city limits (and still it snowed). We were met by a delegation from Eleusis at that point, or we should have been hard put to it to find the way. Ionides later revealed that the ignorant among the Athenian population, and in particular the women, believed that I, the Pythia, had caused the destruction of life in the street, though the better educated saw that it was the work of Pan, whom indeed we had ignored totally, so no wonder. The Eleusinians gave us shelter and fed us, though with an ill grace and some fear. Megara sent an escort for us and made a point of how Athens had neglected us. We could have been attacked on the road, they said. The cold weather was making the brigands very daring.

In the upshot we discovered that the Megarans were not proposing to bring us home by way of their city, but were conducting us as a goatherd might his flock to the countryside boundaries of Corinth, which had already agreed to receive us on the way home as they had received us on the way out. We entered Corinth in a snowstorm and it was an easy matter for our Corinthian friend to accommodate us because we had dwindled to a party of four. The escort sent by Megara was told at the boundary that the Corinthians would receive us but not a single Megaran. In fact, Megara and Corinth were at cross-purposes again: but then, what cities which have a common boundary aren't?

Our wealthy Corinthian friend treated us very kindly. He would not care to have us use the ferry while the pilot was unable to see the farther shore. We were able to bathe in hot water, be massaged and then entertained to a banquet where the music was as exquisite as the food. On returning from the bath I found such a gown laid out on my bed as surely no Pythia ever wore but only, I told myself amusedly, some goddess in a Corinthian heaven. I could not wear it. That would have been unseemly. I was forced therefore to put on a drab robe which was suitable for the oracle. I wished very much that it could have been inspired by the god to give our friend some good luck or promise of long life and high fortune. But he already had the high fortune and I did not think long life was a credible promise to one who lived and ate and drank as he did. It was a pity for though in secret, as he thought, he was a devotee of strange demons and had symbols and even statues of the Olympians round his halls, he was a genuinely religious man and believed in the oracles. He had visited all the most famous ones in the world in the days, as he said, when he could not lay one drachma against another, but with fortune came fat, and with fat, indolence. He was deeply disappointed not to see me wearing his gift. I replied with thanks and said how pleased I should be to see it on a more appropriate person. One course of the meal later he clapped his hands and – behold! – the prettiest girl I have ever seen in my life walked in with a goddess gait, wearing my proffered present, that robe of cloth of gold! 'If,' he said, 'I cannot persuade you, Lady, to wear what is fit for a queen, at least you will not object to receiving a crown.' So then another slave came in, bearing a crown on a cushion. It was one of those delicate gold objects of thin branches with nodding leaves and flowers. I suppose it used no more than an ounce or two of the metal yet contrived by its delicacy to exhibit the very nature and genius of gold without ostentation. I thought that on the appropriate person, an Olympias perhaps, or even Helen, the very beauty of it would reduce the onlookers to tears. I had a sudden thought and it burst out of me, as it was bound to do, in hexameters – how before smoking Ilium Menelaus stood calling for his false wife Helen with his sword in his hand, and how she came from the smoke wearing this crown and the sword fell from his hand. It had become a poem in the extravagant modern manner. The Corinthian was all admiration, asking who had written it. Rashly, and buoyed by the verse, I admitted

169

I had done it myself. I saw Ionides go pale and the Corinthian fall into a silence. I thought to mend matters by explaining that to know how to make hexameters was the only way to prevent the Pythia from being killed by some particularly strong communication. But could the young girl please put on the crown too? So he told her to and of course the sight was beyond admiration. I thought then that the making of this crown was the difference between Hellenes and barbarians, in that the Hellene crafts had crowned a woman with the very spirit of gold rather than the substance of it. But then the Corinthian exclaimed, saying he thought he heard his other guest in the atrium, and who should it be but the secretary of Lucius Galba, saying that his master had been delayed and would arrive later. After he had returned, the Corinthian sent the girl away with her dress and crown and asked after the success of our journey. Ionides had to admit that the return had been disappointing. The Corinthian pressed him for details, and when Ionides rather shamefacedly admitted how much we were short of the required sum he cried out, 'This must not be!'

There and then he sent for his tablets and scribbled on them. He handed them after that to Ionides whose face went even paler, then flushed red.

'This is godlike!'

Just then and quite clearly I heard four words spoken outside the room. I am sure they were part of the service and spoken by some man who had good and sufficient reason to say them, not knowing how they would echo in the banqueting hall.

'It was the ferryman.'

Of course Corinth is the start of the ferry on this particular road to Delphi – indeed there are many roads that start at Corinth, even the sea route for drachmas on their way to Rome. But these words rang in my head and I was as fearful as any countrywoman who sees a raven on the wrong hand. But Ionides handed me the tablets and I saw that the Corinthian had engaged himself to make up the huge sum necessary to repair our roof. Ionides could not express his admiration and gratitude and spoke of his inability in words of such elegance that the Corinthian, his belly shaking with laughter, recommended him to say it in hexameters. There was much meaning running round the banqueting hall like water underground, and he did need a diviner. He was fondling the pretty girl in a way that made me sure she was boughten – indeed, what slaves would such a man have had born in his house – a man of no family? It made me jealous in a curious way, feeling that such beauty ought not to be treated so lightly, though the girl could not object. He let her go, telling her to run along and get out of her finery.

'It is Macedonian work,' he said, 'and very old. It is said to have belonged to the royal family even before the time of the God Alexander the Great.'

I thought to myself: the girl is gold, too, human gold, drawn out thin and fine spun. If he would give me that girl I would look after her as no mother could! But Lucius Galba, the Propraetor of southern Greece, was announced and we all stood up. He came in rather like a piece of storm. Had been delayed by the snow. The fool who guided the ship – it was the ferryman of all people – had said he could not steer a straight course with thick snow round his ears and eyes, though any landsman could have told him there was a steady north-east wind and all he had to do was keep it on the left cheek. He recollected himself and bade us lie down again. We did so as the pallium over the centre of the hall boomed and all the lights fluttered. In fact his stay was brief. He was very respectful to me, not to say servile. The Romans are very superstitious and don't mind showing it. But it was not religious awe. I don't think these western barbarians are capable of that. As soon as he had been served food and drink he dealt with us in a series of abrupt sentences.

'You, Lady, can you be oracular anywhere?'

'No, Propraetor.'

'Why not?'

Ionides slid into this farcical conversation smoothly.

'What oracle can, Propraetor? Would you ask your Sybil of Cumae to leave her cave? Or one of Dodona's oaks to pick up its roots and run to do your bidding? Of course, a Propraetor might command such a thing and I suppose an oak, given the right incentive, might do it – and then there are –'

'Who is this?'

'I was about to make the introductions,' said the Corinthian. 'This is Ionides, the son of Ionides, High Priest of Apollo. *That* is the Pythia of Delphi.'

'It's the first time I've seen a woman reclining like a man rather than sitting.'

'The First Lady,' said Ionides, with ice in his voice, 'is a law unto herself and obeys no one but the god.'

'Not on my patch she doesn't,' said Lucius Galba. 'If she won't prophesy for me, that's her affair. But she'll obey me like the rest of you Greeks. And you – I remember now. You're the pigeon fancier.'

Ionides did not pale but I saw the wine in the kylix he held start to shiver.

'I'm honoured by your interest, Propraetor.'

'It will continue.'

'Music,' said the Corinthian. 'Let's have some music. Music, don't you think?'

It was a boy's voice, lovely and pure as the gold of the girl's crown. It was enough to make me weep. I mastered my tears though, not wishing to be womanish before this blunt barbarian. He for his part fell silent and listened. The song drifted down to a gentle end. When it had plainly finished Lucius Galba nodded.

'You're good entertainers. I've never denied that.'

'What have you actually denied?' said Ionides demurely. 'Tell us that, Propraetor.'

'The right of any man to foment rebellion against a lawful government.'

173

'Ah,' said Ionides, 'precisely. But what is in fact a lawful government? History seems to me to be a series of lawful governments stacked one on top of the other. You can't obey them all, and circumstances force you to obey the latest one. In this case – well, isn't it obvious?'

'I hope so,' said the Propraetor grimly, 'indeed I hope so.'

'Music again,' said the Corinthian. 'Let us have some more music. And ask Melissa to be so good as to come back, will you?'

The boy's voice rose and presently the girl came back, wearing her – my – gold dress and the crown. The Corinthian gave a barely perceptible jerk of his head which sent her to kneel, smiling with I suppose contrived modesty, before the Propraetor. It seemed to me that his eyes bulged. He lifted the kylix to his face and drained it, then held it out behind him.

'Unmixed,' murmured the Corinthian, 'unmixed don't you think?'

'Me too,' said Ionides. 'Let the snow fall. Let it blow. Let it smother.'

Before the song was done, the Propraetor had hauled the girl on to the couch by him. He shared the unmixed wine with her, and the Corinthian beamed and nodded and my head began to turn. She really did have eyes for no one but Lucius Galba. We might not have been present at all. The Corinthian called for more music and dance, and the dancers flung themselves in with somersaults and high

174

jumps and the shawms sounded brazenly, throatily, and I was jealous, a plain old thing whose dignity and sanctity were disregarded among the noise and dancing and drinking and fondling. The boy who had sung was now whispering in Ion's ear. Defiantly I held out my empty kylix behind me. It was taken. Presently it came back, full and darker in colour, unmixed. The man who handed it to me knelt and smiled with wide, white teeth. He was black. It came to me who I was and what I was. I stood up and shouted.

'A libation!'

I spilt the whole kylixful on the floor before my couch. It was a gesture which would have riveted an audience in the theatre but my humiliating confession must be that in the Corinthian's hall it made no impression at all. The dancers went on dancing, the shawms continued to bray, the Propraetor continued to fondle and the boy told Ionides a story which had them both sniggering like dirty children. It was the Corinthian who rescued me. He stood up and came across and led me into the atrium and handed me over to his house dame who showed me where to sleep.

The next morning was chilly but clear. All the hills of Aetolia across the water were white. Our small party assembled. The Propraetor did not go with us to the ferry, leaving that duty to the Corinthian. He said goodbye to us in the atrium. It was by no means a friendly parting. To me he simply said, 'Goodbye, Lady. A safe journey.' But to Ionides his farewell was blunt.

'Goodbye, Ionides, son of Ionides, Priest of Apollo. My advice to you is that you confine yourself strictly to your religious duties.'

I was beginning to understand things. You will think me blind not to have done so before. But one hears of conspiracies and revolts in other places, one does not expect to stumble over the possibility of one among people one knows. The crossing was calm and under oar. I pestered Ionides with anxious questions but to no avail.

'Let it be, Arieka. These things are not for women.'

'Not even for the Pythia?'

'Not even for her – or at least, not where six oarsmen and a pilot are within earshot.'

'What did you think of our ruler?'

'An excellent man in every way. What do you suppose?'

'I wonder if they –'

'What?'

'Nothing. That crown was wonderful. And the girl. To think that such beauty can be bought!'

'The boy was a dirty-minded little bastard.'

'I thought you rather liked him.'

Ionides did not answer but I saw that old wince and shiver about his mouth which told me, knowing him as I did, that it was time to change the subject.

'At least we have the money for the roof.'

'I only hope this snow hasn't made it worse.'

'We shall soon know.'

But in fact we did not soon know. There was much difficulty in getting our sacred cart ashore and more in finding enough horses to get it up the icy road. I even had to walk like a poor woman, and indeed it was fortunate for the exercise warmed me. Had I sat in the wagon as the snow started again and the wind got up, blowing the snow horizontally, I should probably have died.

VIII

When we reached the hall of the Pythias I invited Ionides in with me. Directly the door was shut behind us I sensed something wrong. The wind still blew. It was so. There was a pile of snow in the corner of the hall. Little Menesthia appeared and when she saw me burst into tears. Yes, the roof had fallen in, or some of it. She had not known what to do nor had the house dame. She said Perseus had contrived to get timber and canvas up there but had not been able to have the roof properly blocked off because when anything was moved everything moved. Perseus himself appeared and told us that this was only the half. The roof of the bookroom was giving way. Could we come and see? Ionides left me to settle back into my apartments which I was thankful to see had not suffered, though there was an indefinable feeling of homelessness about them now that I knew the roof was damaged. Quite soon Ionides came back with Perseus and the Foundation's master carpenter. The carpenter said the two jobs would last into the festival season even if the snow held off and gave him a chance to start. As it was, with this weather showing no sign of letting up . . . Ionides questioned him closely and got as much information as he could. He dismissed him, saying he would let him know his decision. Then he said,

'May I join you in your apartments?'

'Of course, Holy One. Menesthia, stop whimpering, child. You may come with us.'

The largest of our braziers was glowing. I warmed my hands at it and dropped my scarf to my neck. Menesthia stood, sniffing. Ionides walked up and down the long way of the atrium.

'Ionides, I have to say this. The decision is mine, you know.'

'What decision?'

'This is the Pythion. I am the Pythia.'

'Of course, dear Lady. I was merely aiming to save you trouble.'

'Well then, I have decided to start as soon as the weather is better.'

'Can you tell him what to do?'

'No. Can you?'

'Do you not see the difficulty? We have enough brought back from Athens to start, but where?'

'On the roof of course!'

'Yes, but which?'

'Take me with you, Ion.'

'Which roof?'

I was silent. Ionides went on.

'You see, the books will suffer. They are fragile. Irreplaceable.'

I was still silent, thinking.

Books. That huge and magnificent roll of names.

'Both the Python and the bookroom must be looked after. Repaired. That is obvious.'

'No.'

'No?'

'It is not obvious.'

'Well then, make it obvious for me.'

'What is Delphi for?'

'The oracle. That, surely, is obvious.'

'Can Delphi exist without the oracle?'

'No.'

'Or the bookroom? I mean, did the oracle do without a bookroom at some time?'

'The oracle was here before writing was invented.'

'I think not. But I cannot imagine that monster which Apollo slew with his arrows didn't have a bookroom. I don't think that as soon as he had slain the monster Apollo said "Let there be a bookroom."'

'I can't bear this – my bookroom!'

'Where you learnt what a power the hexameter could be!'

'Ion – what can we do?'

'The bookroom will have to suffer. We'll try a temporary measure there and hope for better days. I daresay Perseus can shift the books about. When there's a lull we'll go and look.'

183

*

The lull was a long time coming. It seemed the snow would last for ever. I think the climate must have been better when the Pythion and the bookroom were built. But at last the snow ceased to fall, though it lay frozen hard on the ground and the roofs. One of the main reasons for thinking that the Pythion and the bookroom were the oldest buildings in Delphi, except the oracle itself, was that the pitch of those two roofs was different. They were flatter, as if the builders had never supposed they would have to bear the weight of snow. As for the oracle itself, built against and indeed, into the mountain, it was too small for the snow to make much difference. Also, as if Apollo had inspired the builders, the slope of the roof was greater so that the snow slid off.

As soon as the snow had stopped falling we huddled ourselves into outdoor clothes and picked our way the few yards to the bookroom. Perseus received us looking doleful. Indeed, at first sight the damage was terrible. Fortunately, however, we discovered that it was almost all confined to that part of the bookroom which contained the Latin books and which for that reason was called the librarium. The scrolls and codexes, as Ion called some curious blocks of paper, had been removed and stacked at the other end of the bookroom, out of danger. I believe both Ion and I – particularly Ion, I should say – were secretly a little pleased that Apollo should have spared the Greek books but made a real mess of the barbarian Latin ones.

Ion even said as much.

'That'll show them!'

'Ion – Lucius Galba! The Propraetor! He'd be bound to see this put right, for the credit of Rome!'

Ion thought.

'I'm not in good odour. You detected that at least?'

'At least? Your Sanctity is not always very observant. I received a distinct warning from our Lord and Master.'

'Your Holiness was all politeness I thought.'

'Remember the child. Menesthia – aren't you shocked?'

'Oh no, Your Holiness. It's right to call you Holiness, isn't it?'

Ion laughed, then turned to me again.

'But you could write a letter to him, First Lady.'

'I? Write a letter?'

'Why not? If you can read, you can write.'

'I would get Perseus to do it. I could sign it Pythia. The Pythia.'

'You'd far better let me do it. But you'd better practise signing it – I'll think about that – but for a start practise writing the word Pythia. We'll decide later whether you sign it also with your given name.'

'I don't think that would be proper. Besides, someone might use it.'

'For what?'

'Well – you know – magic.'

'We'll think. Can you write, Young Lady? Or do you prefer just being an object?'

'What on earth do you mean, Ion?' I said.

'Do you understand, Young Lady?'

'Yes, Your Holiness,' replied Menesthia, 'of course I do.'

'Do what? Understand or prefer to be an object?'

'Both of course, Your Holiness.'

'You had better explain to me, Ion. I suppose I'm slow-witted.'

'Of course you're not. You just don't think in those terms. Menesthia knows she'd prefer being a pretty girl and wearing pretty clothes to sitting in a bookroom all day looking at dull old books. Right?'

'Yes, Your Holiness.'

'Menesthia! How can you use hexameters if you haven't read them?'

'You're forgetting, Dear Lady. Once you had only heard them, not read them; and even when you read them you spoke them out loud. I heard you.'

'Menesthia, did you sit in the portico as I said you could? While we were away?'

'Yes, First Lady, of course I did. There weren't many enquirers to begin with, but quite a lot came later on after I got known. I used to sit there. Of course I always had Lydia standing behind me –'

'You didn't squat, surely!'

'No, First Lady. I had Lydia carry a milking stool for me and I sat on that. It was quite comfortable, you know, and really rather like being back on the farm. I was well wrapped up of course. It's cold on that portico and I didn't go inside. But I quite enjoyed myself most days. I had my funny feeling to begin with but, you know, later on it wasn't really necessary.'

'But what did you do – say?'

'Well of course when I had my funny feeling I don't know what I said! But later on I realized that it was quite simple. If it's a young man you tell him he'll be lucky in love. If he's old you tell him he will have a long life and some unexpected good fortune is coming his way.'

'The women?'

'There weren't many women.'

'Menesthia. You may go now.'

The girl curtsied and withdrew.

'Somebody will have to take her in hand.'

'Your job, First Lady. I don't envy you.'

'Most men would.'

'Would they? Yes, I suppose so. She's a pretty little' – and again, that wince and shudder – 'thing.'

We were defeated. Menesthia proved as intractable as a wild ass. Even her 'funny times' became less frequent, and I am quite sure that she ended by pretending that she had them. As spring broadened out from the lowlands and climbed the winding road up to Delphi she became pale and tearful and whiny. In the end she begged so hard to go home that we had to let her go for she was a free woman, and her father agreed to take her back, dowry and all. He was soft and entirely unlike my own father. He made me wonder about myself far more than she did. For she was quite easily understood – a spoilt priestess. He on the other hand was a man – little more than a smallholder – who spoilt his animals, let alone his children.

I did wonder about Menesthia's 'funny times'. They made me uneasy because though I had been First Lady for many years I had never experienced anything like them. I needed the smoke of laurel leaves, yet their magic power seemed to lessen. The Olympians seemed to be going farther and farther away. I had become – but by fits and starts – increasingly uneasy about them and in particular Apollo. I had read a great deal by now and was confused. Nobody seemed to know precisely who the Olympians were and whether Apollo had originally been one of them. I communicated this unease to Ion who had very little counsel to give. He said to go on as I was and hope that there would be light shed by the gods themselves. In addition to this worry there was the question of some girl to select as a possible Second Lady, for, as I said to Ion, I was not going to live for ever.

'Dear Lady! Will not the oracle look after itself?'

'I wish I could be sure of that.'

'If you are not, who is?'

'You of course!'

Ion gave me a long, critical look.

In the end we repaired the roof of the Pythion properly and left the sodden corner of the bookroom, which had been the librarium, remain 'a temporary solution'. It did mean that the whole great room was colder and Perseus complained that he would snuffle the whole year round. But as I told him, what would Delphi be without a Pythia and he had to agree.

Phocis sent us a girl. She was a skinny little thing and we caught her at the moment when she was about to shoot up, which she did. She was dark as I was and called Meroe. I think she had some connection with Egypt. She was a solemn creature and extremely pious. Indeed, I made up my mind that I would not be intimidated by her piety, but I never quite succeeded in ridding myself of the feeling that she disapproved of her First Lady. She had no 'funny feelings' but did not think she should learn to read until Serapis indicated that she should. Serapis was a new god, not one of the old Egyptian ones, and it made me uneasier still. If we were about the business of inventing gods where would it end?

Then Ionides disappeared. It was some time before I noticed that he was missing, having got so used to his presence I supplied it unconsciously even when he was not there. There was a confusion when I went to the tripod to utter the oracular response and realized that Ion wasn't there. In the end one of the Holy Ones stood in for him but I had to prompt him for he could not manage the hexameters. It was not edifying. People had begun to expect the verse form from me and, though I used it, this untrained young man gave out a lame version in prose. So what some people were kind enough to call 'the revival of the oracle' suffered a setback as they say. I was eager for

Ionides to return. I had learnt to lean on him. Then I discovered that Perseus had been missing, too. I learnt this because he asked to see me and confessed that he had been absent.

'Why?'

'I went with His Holiness, First Lady.'

'Where?'

'Epirus.'

'But – I think you had better explain.'

So it all came out. The information gathering, the speed of communication, the couriers, the whole organization I had thought was for the support of the oracle, had been turned by Ion and some of the Holy Ones into a plot against the Romans. I do not expect anyone who has bothered to read this far to credit the situation. But Delphi and some of the lesser-known oracles were trying to persuade mainland Greece to shake itself free from Roman rule! What made the whole scheme preposterous was that there was nothing wrong with Roman rule! Of course there are rotten apples in any barrel, but the Romans were giving Greece what she had never been able to give herself. For hundreds of years mainland Greece had been nothing but a collection of large villages fighting each other with every kind of trickery and treachery and savagery. Now there was the rule of law and peace. Of course the Romans made us pay cash for it, but we were glad, too. Even now when it looks as if the Romans themselves are going to have a civil war and fight it out in our country rather than their own, the situation is more peaceful than it was in the days when every village thought it had a holy duty to fight its neighbour. I used to think – but privately – that we should have avoided two hundred years of bickering if the Persians had only conquered us the way the Romans did. And now here was Ionides of all people meeting conspiratorially in Epirus with other madmen against the most powerful country in the world!

Not that the conspiracy got very far. There was a certain pathos about it. Perseus – whom Ion had just ordered to go along without telling him more than 'he needed to know' – Perseus told me what happened. They reached the place where they were supposed to meet with the other conspirators – passwords and all – and no one was there. They waited, sitting on a rock in the middle of nowhere and examining the future by means of birdwatching. The future was exceptionally favourable it appeared. But then what appeared was Romans who rose, apparently out of the ground, and arrested them both. They were searched in a most humiliating and unnecessary way, for Ionides was not carrying anything and Perseus was carrying some food and all the relevant papers in a leather bag. A further humiliation, said Perseus, was that the officer in charge wasn't even a colonel. But they knew everything – why the other conspirators were not there, who they were and what the plan was. The Romans had been – to use a Latin word for which Greek has no exact equivalent – efficient.

'I know I'm a slave,' said Perseus, 'and I was resigning myself to the probability of being tortured since they couldn't torture His Holiness. Even so I have my pride and it was the last humiliation when they told me to run along.'

'They let you go!'

'I'm afraid so.'

'How could you leave him?'

'Indeed, First Lady, I did all the things you read about. You know – faithful slave stuff – but it didn't work. Even when I tried to follow they prodded me in the tum with the butt end of a spear.'

'They took him away –'

'The last I heard of him he was declaiming. He said he was in the hands of god. The officer said, "Come, sir, Your Holiness, it's not as bad as that!"'

'Oh – what shall I do?'

'It's not for me to say, First Lady. I shall go back to the bookroom which I should never have left.'

He paused in his going and turned to me again.

'He said to give you this.'

It was a silver key, but of an extraordinary shape. The two ends were each shaped as a labrys, the Cretan double axe. But this was doubly doubled.

'Which end is which?'

'I don't know, Lady. I thought you would. The officer was most respectful of it, wouldn't touch it. Oh, every courtesy as they say, after they'd searched us.'

I had no idea what to do with the key, or even if it was more than symbolic. I threaded a silver chain round the barrel to remind myself what it was and put it away. What to do? It was an ideal moment for the obvious recourse – ask the oracle of Delphi! But how can a Pythia ask herself a question and then transmit to herself the god's answer, if, if – if there is a god to give the answer? I thought to myself, the seven wise men of Greece might well be asked in vain for an answer to that situation. Even in my anxiety for Ion I could not but think the situation unique and in a rueful kind of way, amusing. Nevertheless I was drawn towards the building. I veiled myself and stole along to it. The great doors set back in the colonnade whined loudly as I pushed one leaf open enough to let me through. Here it was, the steps down, the niches in the wall, each for a Holy One, and the last niche for the holiest of all, the High Priest of Apollo, his Holiness the Warden of the Holy Ones. There was the tripod, by it, the brazier, empty now, since the seventh day of the month was past. There beyond and behind the tripod were the curtains, the drawstrings hanging down the right-hand side. A stiff, not to say crude image of Apollo woven into the stuff of the left-hand curtain faced some misshapen monster in the right. As always they made the goose pimples rise on my skin, and the rhythm of my breathing quickened. It was a holy place, the most holy in Greece, most holy in the world. I tried to explain this to myself, said to myself that I was the Pythia faced with temptation. No. I was Arieka, the little barbarian afraid of the dark. But dark herself, oh yes. I went on tiptoe through the dusk of the adyton and stood close to the curtain, so close I felt my breath might stir it – and had a convulsion of pure fear when I thought that my breath might lend the monster breath and he/she start into life and overwhelm me. I did not think of Apollo in the other curtain but only of the monster, surely now stirring into life. I began to back away, keeping my eye on him, and presently he stilled and my breathing slowed and I knew some woman had woven him and woven the god, some woman of flesh and blood, even a Pythia perhaps, instructed by the god to make this image of him and the darkness he had faced.

Let it be. Let the curtains hang there. Apollo send Ionides back to me! He is more than a husband, that quicksilver, quicksand, learned mountebank of the gods! I believe in him, liar, soothsayer, self-deceiver, fool, the eighth wise man –

Well, Arieka, what did you expect?

A god, that's what you expected.

They turned their backs on you.

They vanished and there was grief before the void. The Void.

Presently I came out of that unprofitable feeling and found myself walking down the street, my face bare and people looking strangely at me. So with an automatic gesture I veiled myself and entered the Pythion.

He was sitting on one of the chairs like a woman. Or

like an ancient statue. His eyes were shut.

'Ion. Ionides, oh you, you fool. You moron, you, you –'

'Get up, for god's sake. No, not that. Just get up. Stop wetting my feet. I've had enough. I shall kill myself –'

'Ion –'

'I know, I know. Imagine. They let me go. Lucius Galba, that Roman bastard. He let me go. He said the secret of Roman Power was that it robbed men of their dignity. Then they were nothing. Oh God, the Father of Gods and Men, strike him blind! Apollo spill his seed with your arrow – Artemis freeze his bed – You demons that I called up, torment him!'

'Ion –'

The strange man clasped himself with his arms and began to chant.

'Ion. Ion. Ion. Ion. Ion. Ion –'

Then I knew what he was doing. He was finding a place to hide, to draw into and away from himself, his shame the last bit of clothing to be dropped before the void, where at last there is the peace of not-god, not-man – nothingness –

'Ion. Ion. Ion –'

Suddenly he stopped. He wiped his eyes and stood up. Spoke briskly.

'Well, that's that, then.'

He stood, looking down at me.

'Well, Pythia. That's that. You don't understand do you? You with your knack of suffering. I can't. I mean I can for a bit, like just now and before you came in. Real, genuine – shame. And now it's over. That's the difference between us.'

'You're back –'

'No I'm not.'

So that was how His Holiness came home. But, as he said, he wasn't home. And the little that had really come did not last long. I saw him dwindle. Presently it became plain that he would dwindle right away. I asked the god if it was possible for him to live. And I knew what the god's answer was, for it was the same as my own. I had taken, indeed, not to addressing an Apollo out there – somewhere in the empyrean it may be – but that woman's image, as a child would. So I suppose that at last the Pythia did indeed answer herself.

Perseus said something acute.

'If His Holiness was a slave he would live.'

I saw that was true; and it was in a way a compliment to Ion, so I passed it on to him. He laughed crazily when he heard it.

'Perseus thinks there is a man in here!'

'So there is, Ion. Be a man.'

'You lack conviction. How wonderful, though, if something real like dying because I had lost my dignity actually happened to me! No, no, my dear. I shall totter on, growing senile and finding not death but oblivion. You may have the leavings burnt.'

That is what happened more or less. He did become silly, not in the way he always had been at times, but a silliness without any wisdom in it. There was oblivion and presently his body died. I did not suffer with him because as so often in these cases of extreme age he had really died a long time before.

The day his body died I went and sat in his niche for the first time in my life and, I think, the last time. There was nothing. He did not come back. It seemed to me that with his death, though I was the Pythia with a Second Lady ready to take over my duties, nevertheless with Ion the oracle died. I let her go through the motions. I understood that old First Lady I had known so many years ago. Sixty? More, I think. I have lost count. But the world has changed. Sixty will do.

When the winter came and the Second Lady ceased giving oracles and the young man who sat in Ion's niche had ceased interpreting her noises for the questioner – when, I say, that deadly wind blew down and sifted the unmelting snow along the cobbled street, I returned to the oracle, as was my right, and opened one leaf of the door. I passed through the colonnade, down the steps past the niches, round the tripod and stood before the curtains. The key with the double labrys was hanging round my neck. I pulled the drawstrings slowly and the curtains slid back. There was a double door behind them. I stood before it for a long time but the only thought that came to me was that whatever happened it did not matter much. So I put the silver labrys into the silver lock and turned the key. The doors were easy enough to open. There was the solid, impenetrable rock of the mountain behind them.

It was only the next day that I received a letter from the Archon of Athens. In view of my long service as Pythia of the Apolline Oracle the city wished to erect a stone image of me among the altars on the Field of Mars. I wrote back – remembering the void – and feeling strangely that there was a kind of tenderness in it that I could explain to nobody. I asked that rather than an image of me they should erect a simple altar and inscribe there:

TO THE UNKNOWN GOD

The novels of William Golding

ff

Lord of the Flies

A plane crashes on a desert island and the only survivors, a group of schoolboys, assemble on the beach and wait to be rescued. By day they inhabit a land of bright fantastic birds and dark blue seas, but at night their dreams are haunted by the image of a terrifying beast. As the boys' delicate sense of order fades, so their childish dreams are transformed into something more primitive, and their behaviour starts to take on a murderous, savage significance.

ff

The Inheritors

This was a different voice; not the voice of the people.
It was the voice of other.

When the spring came the people moved back to their familiar home. But this year strange things were happening – inexplicable sounds and smells; unexpected acts of violence; and new, unimaginable creatures half glimpsed through the leaves. Seen through the eyes of a small tribe of Neanderthals whose world is hanging in the balance, *The Inheritors* explores the emergence of a new race, *Homo sapiens*, whose growing dominance threatens an entire way of life.

ff

Pincher Martin

Drowning in the freezing North Atlantic, Christopher Hadley Martin, temporary lieutenant, happens upon a grotesque rock, an island that appears only on weather charts. To drink there is a pool of rain water; to eat there are weeds and sea anemones. Through the long hours with only himself to talk to, Martin must try to assemble the truth of his fate, piece by terrible piece. *Pincher Martin* is a terrifying and unforgettable journey into one man's mind.

ff

Free Fall

Somehow, somewhere, Sammy Mountjoy lost his freedom, the faculty of freewill 'that cannot be debated but only experienced, like a colour or the taste of potatoes'. As he retraces his life in an effort to discover why he no longer has the power to choose and decide for himself, the narrative moves between England and a prisoner-of-war camp in Germany. In *Free Fall*, his fourth novel, William Golding has created a poetic fiction, and an allegory, as moving as it is unforgettable.

ff

The Spire

Dean Jocelin has a vision: that God has chosen him to erect a great spire on his cathedral. His mason anxiously advises against it, for the old cathedral was built without foundations. Nevertheless, the spire rises octagon upon octagon, pinnacle by pinnacle, until the stone pillars shriek and the ground beneath it swims. Its shadow falls ever darker on the world below, and on Dean Jocelin in particular.

ff

The Pyramid

Oliver is eighteen, and wants to enjoy himself before going to university. But this is the 1920s, and he lives in Stilbourne, a small English country town, where everyone knows what everyone else is getting up to, and where love, lust and rebellion are closely followed by revenge and embarrassment. Written with great perception and subtlety, *The Pyramid* is William Golding's funniest and most light-hearted novel, which probes the painful awkwardness of the late teens, the tragedy and farce of life in a small community and the consoling power of music.

ff

The Scorpion God

Three short novels show Golding at his subtle, ironic, mysterious best. In *The Scorpion God* we see the world of ancient Egypt at the time of the earliest pharaohs. *Clonk Clonk* is a graphic account of a crippled youth's triumph over his tormentors in a primitive matriarchal society. And *Envoy Extraordinary* is a tale of Imperial Rome where the emperor loves his illegitimate grandson more than his own arrogant, loutish heir.

ff

Darkness Visible

Darkness Visible opens at the height of the London Blitz, when a naked child steps out of an all-consuming fire. Miraculously saved but hideously scarred, soon tormented at school and at work, Matty becomes a wanderer, a seeker after some unknown redemption. Two more lost children await him, twins as exquisite as they are loveless. Toni dabbles in political violence; Sophy, in sexual tyranny. As Golding weaves their destinies together, his book reveals both the inner and outer darkness of our world.

ff

The Paper Men

Fame, success, fortune, a drink problem slipping over the edge into alcoholism, a dead marriage, the incurable itches of middle-aged lust. For Wilfred Barclay, novelist, the final unbearable irritation is Professor Rick L. Tucker, implacable in his determination to become The Barclay Man. Locked in a lethal relationship they stumble across Europe, shedding wives, self-respect and illusions. The climax of their odyssey, when it comes, is as inevitable as it is unexpected.

ff

Rites of Passage

Sailing to Australia in the early years of the nineteenth century, Edmund Talbot keeps a journal to amuse his godfather back in England. Full of wit and disdain, he records the mounting tensions on the ancient, sinking warship where officers, sailors, soldiers and emigrants jostle in the cramped spaces below decks. Then a single passenger, the obsequious Reverend Colley, attracts the animosity of the sailors, and in the seclusion of the fo'castle something happens to bring him into a 'hell of degradation', where shame is a force deadlier than the sea itself.

ff

Close Quarters

In a wilderness of heat, stillness and sea mists, a ball is held on a ship becalmed halfway to Australia. In this surreal, fête-like atmosphere the passengers dance and flirt, while beneath them thickets of weed like green hair spread over the hull. The sequel to *Rites of Passage*, *Close Quarters*, the second volume in Golding's acclaimed sea trilogy, is imbued with his extraordinary sense of menace. Half-mad with fear, with drink, with love and opium, everyone on this leaky, unsound hulk is 'going to pieces'. And in a nightmarish climax the very planks seem to twist themselves alive as the ship begins to come apart at the seams.

ff

Fire Down Below

The third volume of William Golding's acclaimed sea trilogy. A decrepit warship sails on the last stretch of its voyage to Sydney Cove. It has been blown off course and battered by wind, storm and ice. Nothing but rope holds the disintegrating hull together. And after a risky operation to reset its foremast with red-hot metal, an unseen fire begins to smoulder below decks.

ff

The Double Tongue

Golding's final novel, left in draft at his death, tells the story of a priestess of Apollo. Arieka is one of the last to prophesy at Delphi, in the shadowy years when the Romans were securing their grip on the tribes and cities of Greece. The plain, unloved daughter of a local grandee, she is rescued from the contempt and neglect of her family by her Delphic role. Her ambiguous attitude to the god and her belief in him seem to move in parallel with the decline of the god himself – but things are more complicated than they appear.